THE MIDNIGHT LINE MYSTERY

THE MIDNIGHT LINE MYSTERY

by Dorothy Parker

Illustrated by Anne Wood B.A.

TUPS Books

Published by TUPS Books
30 Lime Street, Newcastle upon Tyne NE1 2PQ
Tel: 0191-233 0990 Fax: 0191-233 0578

Typeset by Sumner Type, London SE22
Printed by Trade Union Printing Services, Newcastle upon Tyne

A C.I.P. catalogue record for this book is available from the
British Library

ISBN

For my Husband, who set the wheels in motion

What might have been the Midnight Line is now a public footpath, with a stretch of narrow-gauge railway run by the STRPS from Alston. So, it is possible to follow in the tracks of this railway-orientated story.

Duggy's 0-4-0 referred to in the book has now moved to the Tanfield Railway in Co. Durham, the nearest standard-gauge line from Slaggyford, where it is under restoration and will operate on that railway.

D. Parker

1

The school van pulled in behind a parked Range Rover to let
out Cathy, Duggy and Simon and it was not in Simon's nature
to miss the chance of a close look at this latest model. He
walked round it, anorak hooked over one finger and dangling
down his back; then he paused and pressed his face against
the front offside window, hand cupped over his eyes the
better to inspect the dashboard, when a furious voice shouted
from the Post Office doorway.

'Hey you—what d'ye think you're doing? Clear off! Snotty-nosed brats—go on, the lot of you, clear off!'

Instinctively, Cathy and Duggy had cleared off when they noticed the shop door opening. Simon joined them, but before he had time to catch his breath the driver climbed into the Rover, shut the door, started up and made off down the road.

Cathy leaned against the stone wall of the pinfold, wiping her eyes on the ends of her school scarf. 'If you could've seen your face, Si!' she gasped, still laughing. 'Snotty-nosed brats!'

Simon flushed and swiped at Cathy with his anorak. 'Well, I didn't see him coming out of the shop, did I? Didn't even touch his rotten car anyway—and you can shut up too—it's not all that funny.'

'It was from over here! Wonder what he's doing round here anyway—he didn't exactly match his posh car,' Cathy said thoughtfully, flinging her scarf-ends round her neck, in opposite directions. 'I don't like him though.'

'I don't like him, or his driving, or anything that is his—doesn't deserve a car like a Rover—foot through the floorboards practically before the handbrake was off.'

'Oh, come on, you two. It's only a car and my tea'll be ready,' Duggy called over his shoulder. 'Should all be banned, I reckon.'

'I thought you liked your food too much to want to ban teas. Just look at him!' Cathy laughed unkindly, pointing at Duggy's rear as she followed him up the road out of the village, towards the level-crossing.

'Ignore her, Duggy—everybody else does. Hullo! What's this then? Finished painting your shunter, eh? All ready for the big day . . . doesn't look bad—'

They stopped, leaning on the stone dyke to look beyond the newly dug garden, over to the station yard, where the LNER-green 0-4-0 tank engine stood on a short length of track in the yard, so close to the north end of the house that it looked like an extension.

Duggy looked pleased at Simon's unusual show of interest. 'Aye, she's ready for a boiler test, then we'll take her up to Alston—handy for shunting and that, once the line's open again.' He went on enthusiastically. 'Did I mention about somebody donating an old railmotor? Needs a bit done to it, but now that yon tank engine's finished—' He gestured towards the 0–4–0. 'I'll have time to get on with the railmotor. It might be coming tomorrow, if they can get somebody to lend them a lorry, but in any case it'll be here for the weekend. The ALPS lot at Alston are busy getting ready up there for the reopening, though, so I'll just get on with it down here.'

Simon yawned loudly. He was not the keenest of railway fans, or fanatics as he called them.

They continued up the road, slowing as they approached the Station House door.

'Won't be long now, Duggy till your big day. May Day's opening day, isn't it? I say, Duggy—' Cathy lowered her voice. 'Has your dad finished his new loco yet? You know—' She nodded significantly, so that her thick dark hair swung out round her head. 'Up at Alston—the secret one...'

Duggy frowned and walked smartly up to the door without speaking. Then: 'See you,' he said tersely, not looking at the others. And he slammed the door.

'Well!' Cathy stared at the still-quivering door-knocker. 'What's got into him? Duggy's not usually huffy.'

'It's supposed to be hush-hush, you idiot. The new loco, I mean. I told you that. "Not a word", I said, and here you are blabbing. Remember I told you not to let on to anybody about Big Duggy's loco?' Simon said. 'Well, you just did! And young Duggy's upset 'cos you're not supposed to know about it. And now he knows that I've told you. And step on it, can't you?'

'Well, but Duggy's nobody—I mean, it's his engine anyway! His dad's, at least – and I only said "was it finished?" That's not going to do any harm, is it? Anyway, you shouldn't have told me if you didn't want me to know! And what's all the fuss about, anyway—it's only a steam engine or something. It's not going to grab any headlines, is it? "Steam-engine driver builds steam engine." Ha!'

'I'll know what to do the next time anybody I know builds the prototype of a super new type of loco.' Simon stopped to glare at Cathy. 'Listen, it's special—Big Duggy designed it and made it, and he doesn't want anybody to know too much about it till it's launched on May Day.' He shrugged. 'Just forget about it and hurry up. Mum'll have kittens if we're late again and lambing not finished.'

'Well, I like that! Everybody at school knows what's going on—Jo's dad works at the foundry where they cast the wheels, and she told me about it before you did. So there!' Cathy's voice rose indignantly as she trotted to keep up with her brother's long strides. 'Slow down a bit, will you, Si? I'm out of puff!'

Simon shortened his stride slightly. 'Pipe down, can't you? You've got a voice like a fog-horn—the whole parish'll have heard you rabbiting on. And don't forget—in future, the fewer folk know about Unicus being so special the better. It could mean a lot of work for the foundries, you know—it's big business, all that casting and stuff'll mean there'll be a lot of jobs. And that's why Big Duggy doesn't want it splattered all over the newspapers and people crawling all over the engine-sheds before the opening day. There's a lot of experts coming to see the loco performing,' he said vaguely; and after a pause he added quietly: 'But he'll go berserk if he finds out Duggy told me about it—or anybody . . .'

Cathy stopped dead and stared at Simon. 'Industrial sabotage! Wow—that's what you're on about, isn't it? Big

Duggy's worried in case somebody pinches his invention. A big firm—or foreigners might be interested—a Foreign Power, mebbe, if it's all that good. That's what you mean, isn't it?'

Simon nodded and thought: 'Oh no—she's done it again'

'Well, why the heck can't you say so instead of treating me like an idiot?' Cathy exploded. 'Just 'cos I'm your sister doesn't mean I'm mentally deficient!'

Defeated, Simon sprinted ahead, up the dusty fell road and through the gate on to the narrow, rough, even dustier track which sloped sharply down to a hump-back bridge over a fast-moving burn: the Haugh Burn. Burnhaugh farmhouse and its ancient pattern of buildings lay over the bridge and to the left, in a sheltered hollow surrounded by greening fells. Ewes and their lambs scampered off the track, panic-stricken at the sudden noise and movement as Cathy and Simon galloped down the home stretch, into the cobbled yard.

2

The following Saturday morning Simon came yawning into the kitchen just as the phone rang; he raced Cathy to answer it.

Duggy's excited voice rang out: 'It's here, Si! The rail-motor's here. It's great—fancy coming down to look it over?'

'Five minutes,' Simon said, going straight to the point. He dropped the receiver and snatched his anorak from behind the back door.

'Well—seen it's Duggy—he doesn't need a phone—not for short distances like under five miles,' Cathy said, still smarting from Duggy's odd behaviour.

'You coming or not?' Simon asked impatiently, hovering in the doorway. 'Hurry up if you are, 'cos Dad's just coming into the yard and he'll give us something to do if he finds us doing nothing.'

'Course I'm coming! Just try and stop me. And anyway I haven't just crawled downstairs—I've finished my Saturday jobs and some of yours—like cleaning the hen-house out.' She grinned at Simon's guilty expression. 'I'll tell Mum we're going, and catch you up.'

Mrs. Tate was kneeling on the sitting-room floor in a welter of crumpled newspapers, piles of china and packing cases. She looked up enquiringly as Cathy put her head round the door. 'I'll never be finished in time for opening day—don't bother me now, there's a good lass. All this stuff's to sort and price and repack ready to take down to the shop when somebody has a minute. Then there's an auction sale ... Did you want something or have you just come to rummage? Now where's my marking pen?'

Cathy took in the general air of chaos; her mother's hair always turned frizzy and stuck up round her head when she was in a state.

Her hair was sticking up now; a good sign, really, Cathy considered. It showed that after weeks of putting off, Mum was getting to grips with doing something about her antiques shop, which was due to open at Alston on the same day as the railway.

'And it's no use offering to help—I've got to do it myself, else I'll not know what I've got. If you're going off with Duggy and those Cubby twins, mind what you get up to. I mean, don't get up to anything! Oh—before you go—look at these.' Mrs. Tate held up two porcelain figurines for Cathy to admire. 'Pretty, aren't they?'

'Oh, Mum, they're lovely! What are they?' Cathy cradled one of the fragile pieces in both hands. 'This one's a shepherdess—she's got a lamb under one arm.'

'And this one's a sailor. See how fine the porcelain is—' Mrs. Tate held up the figure to the light, to show Cathy the shadow of her hand through the fine biscuit-ware. 'Don't think I can bear to part with these. It was a good house sale yesterday—all good saleable stuff.'

Cathy laughed as she handed back the shepherdess. 'If you go on like this you'll never sell anything! It's no use having an antique shop if you're going to keep all the best things for yourself.'

Mrs. Tate smiled ruefully as she rewrapped the ornaments. 'Mm, I know what you mean and I've just got to make a profit out of this business—show your Dad that I can do it—I've gone on at him long enough for him to rent the shop, so now it's up to me.'

Mother and daughter exchanged understanding glances, both quick to smile and good-tempered, looking remarkably alike, in spite of their different hair colouring: Cathy's dark and shining; her mother's light and curly.

'We're biking down to Duggy's now. He's got an old railmotor or something to do up. Somebody's given it to ALPS—that's the railway lot, you know. It just came this morning, I think, and he's all excited about it.' Cathy zipped up her anorak. 'Dunno when we'll be back—you know Duggy.'

Mrs. Tate nodded. 'He's really keen on this railway, isn't he?' She found the pen and began looking for the invoice. 'Well, off you go—and mind you don't get into mischief.'

Cathy closed the door quietly behind her. Mum was never going to forget about last year; she still imagined that sheep-rustlers were going to kidnap her and Si every time they set foot outside the house. Then there was the Dice affair, last Christmas. In spite of her vague appearance, her mum, Cathy knew, didn't miss much . . .

From behind a shelter of hay bales Ridley Tate looked up as his daughter cycled, far too fast, out of the yard and over the bridge, scattering hens, ducks and cats as she went. He opened his mouth to shout, 'You'll put the hens off the lay!' then thought better of it and turned his attention back to the ewe, which had produced twin lambs and was nuzzling them affectionately. At least the lambing was going well, he thought, even if other things were not. Simon seemed to be more interested in engines than he was in farming. Contradictious, bairns were, he sighed. You just never knew how they would turn out.

Cathy and Simon met Duggy tacking up the station bank on his bike. His round face was scarlet with effort; he panted.

"Lo, Duggy!' Cathy said loudly, standing with one foot planted either side of her bike. 'Who hasn't stuck to his diet then? Honestly! You sound like Puffing Billy.' Her hazel eyes sparkled as she mentally weighed and measured Duggy's stocky figure. 'And what's this in your pocket? Chocolate?'

Duggy ran a grubby hand over his tightly-curled fair hair; his light blue eyes almost disappeared as his face creased in a grin, all huffiness gone. He never quite knew with Cathy; she embarrassed him sometimes, teasing him. Always good for a laugh, though . . .

Cathy tweaked the bar from his boiler-suit pocket and transferred it to hers, having first wiped it on her jeans.

'I'll look after it for you,' she said, half-disappointed that Duggy had not risen to her teasing, half-glad that he was in a good mood. Cathy enjoyed short dramas, but couldn't bear sulks.

'When you've finished wittering on,' Simon said mildly, 'we'll get on down to the station and take a look at the railmotor. Like before dark, you know.'

Cathy opened her mouth, then shut it.

As they remounted their bicycles a bank of mist began to creep up the Tyne valley from the north.

Cathy shivered. 'Creepy, isn't it? Like a ghostly army on the march. You wouldn't think there was a river there at all—and look, down yonder—you can just see the church spire and a few tree-tops poking through the mist—like one of those Christmas scenes after the snow's settled. And it was a fine spring morning when I got up—birds singing and twittering like mad and everything green and new.'

Duggy nodded without looking at the view; it was easiest to agree with Cathy, but his mind was on the railway and nothing else. 'Hope the weather's not changing altogether—the VIPs won't see anything if it's foggy on Monday. We've got all sorts of folk coming for the opening—did I mention them?'

'There'll be the Transport Minister, rail company chairman,

local gentry, as Grandad calls them, councillors, local MPs, the Society committee, conservationists—the lot! Still, they'll be OK in the observation coach, even if it does rain—the ALPS working party's done a brilliant job on it—all varnished and Brassoed as good as new. And the old loco, the Daler, the one that's going to be first to run on the reopened line—you'd swear it was brand new. Seen them yet?'

Simon shook his head, watching the approaching wedge of fog widening and filling the valley.

'But what Dad's really chuffed about—' Duggy began enthusiastically then stopped, his mouth tight with vexation. 'I mean—'

'Duggy,' Simon interrupted quietly. 'It's OK. Really—I mean about you not being able to tell us much about—well—you know—Unicus and all that. I did sort of mention it to Cathy . . . ' He looked sideways at his sister, who took no notice. 'You know what she's like when she starts—she can get anything out of anybody—but she's not going to be able to talk to many people between now and Monday, so there'll be no more blabbing from us.'

Duggy flushed. 'Well, I did promise Dad I wouldn't mention his invention to anybody—but anyway, I think they've asked him to drive the first scheduled train on the line since BR closed it. S'ppose it's because he drove the last DMUs in 1976, as well as the steam engines way back in the fifties. You know what? Dad's been staying up at Alston at nights for a week or two—sleeping on the footplate of the Daler, or so Mum reckons—in case somebody tries to pinch his brasses!'

They all laughed. Big Duggy, a BR driver and railway fanatic, came of a long line of drivers and fanatics

Cathy preferred to describe such people as railway lunatics 'I can imagine he's keeping an eye on the Daler—as well as sleeping on the hotplate of his new engine. What did you call it? Unicorn? New engines always seem to have funny names, don't they—like Nonpareil. He'll have his peaked cap down over his left ear and his feet in a heap of ashes. You always know what mood Big Duggy's in by the way his cap's on—straight on, with the peak right down over his eyebrows, then look out.' Cathy giggled, then her expression changed as they reached the level-crossing and skidded to a standstill with much squealing of brakes.

'Is that it? Your railmotor?' she exclaimed, pointing over to the left, beyond the station house. 'That rusty old thing?'

They propped their bicycles against the back wall of the platform, jumped down on to the track and hopped across the lines to the siding, where a dilapidated railmotor rested.

'Well you didn't expect Nigel Gresley, did you?' Duggy snapped. His ears turned red. 'We got it given—for no-thing—as in free—at least ALPS did, and they, or we, are doing it up, so's they can use it for taking working parties up and down the line.'

'But I thought it was one of those bus things, like they had on that line in Yorkshire. But that's just a— a—' Words failed her.

'A heap?' Simon suggested. 'And by the way, you lost two points for saying hotplate and Unicorn instead of footplate and Unicus. Where was I now? Ah yes—you've forgotten, Cath—when you were just about this high—' Simon held his arm out about a foot from the ground. 'Big Duggy had one of those railmotor things on the line and took us all on a midnight ride. There was a load of us—the Cubbys, the Robsons, Duggy, us. It was after the line closed officially, so it must have been absolutely the last thing to travel on it before they lifted the track.'

'Really?' Cathy brightened, staring at the railmotor, assessing its possibilities. 'Wish I could remember . . . That's the trouble with doing interesting things when you're young—they're wasted 'cos you forget. How come you can remember and I can't? You're not that much older than I am. It's not fair!'

'Look, Cath, you don't need to remember—it's all here again—we've got a working railway again. Nobody ever thought they would raise enough funds to reopen from scratch—but here we are with re-laid track, rolling-stock, buildings done up, the observation coaches, the Daler and everything. Then there's Dad's Unicus . . . '

Simon yawned noisily. He wondered if Duggy wasn't overdoing the railway bit. He was almost ranting . . . and, after all, you could get from A to B just as well in a decent car—like that Range Rover . . .

Just then a large hand thumped him between the shoulder-blades.

'Tim and Chas—you great oafs,' Simon gasped, pretending to reel back from the blow.

The Cubby twins had, unnoticed, climbed the stile at the south side of the crossing. Chas's large brown eyes looked mournful. Mist sparkled on his long, dark brown spaniel's-ears hair.

'Not you, Chas—him! You'll do somebody an injury some day, Tim Cubby, thumping about like that.'

'No show without Punch!' Tim grinned. 'You should keep your wits about you, lad. Didn't know we were here, did you? Thought we would brighten your dreary day a bit—as little as we can do, really.' Eyeing the railmotor, he went on: 'Is this it, then? Looks OK. Well, at least it's not bad—well, actually, it's a mess. Useful, though, for pottering about.' He patted a panel gently—for him. 'Working order?'

Duggy nodded. 'Aye, just about. I've checked it over. Battery's a bit dodgy—or mebbe it's the ignition. But Dad reckons it'll travel up to Alston sheds under its own steam—if you see what I mean—then the ALPS lads'll paint it up when they get time.'

'Meanwhile, down at Slaggyford station,' Tim murmured, 'our intrepid lads . . . '

'No!' Duggy shouted. 'You're not going to mess it about.'

'Did I say anything?' Tim waved his arms about. 'Did I?'

'Can I just say something?' Cathy asked demurely. 'I mean I know you don't ever really want me to, 'cos you think I cramp your style. But I *am* interested, you know—in trains and things. I say, Chas, I can hardly bear it when your eyes go all sort of luminous and injured, like our cat's when you tread on her tail . . . '

'Go on, for Pete's sake!' Simon said, exasperated; he groaned at the prospect of a whole day's music-hall turns, performed by Cathy and Tim.

'She is,' Chas murmured, 'going on—'.

'Who are we to prevent you? Feel free, dear child. If you have something to say—say it without let or hindrance . . . ' Tim said, with an elaborate bow.

'Don't start, you two', Simon groaned, adding under his breath: 'Lunatics'

'Well,' Cathy said briskly. 'How did the railmotor get here?'

'Fell off the back of a lorry.' Tim said. 'Next question?'

'Can I just—sit on it?'

'No!'

'Can you Cubbys remember me being on that last midnight ride years ago, on a railmotor like this one?'

'Oh, you mean that last ride—when your Mum said you were too little and you'd fall off and you should be in bed anyway, only you howled so much they let you go. You might've fallen off, too. You still might—you haven't grown all that much . . . No, I can't remember that.'

Cathy stuck out her tongue at Tim and sat down at the railmotor controls.

'Looks easy to drive.' She looked at the others significantly, watching their expressions change as they realised . . .

Tim looked interested; he grinned, ready for anything.

Chas, surprised, put his eyebrows up in the middle, like inverted Vs.

Simon weighed up the situation, narrowing his eyes and glancing quickly at the others.

Duggy looked apprehensive—this was worse even than having Tim tinker with the engine

'No!' he croaked. 'We can't drive it yet. Not on the main line—Dad'll go mad.'

'Oh, come on. It's not as if you don't know how to drive. And the line's not actually open yet, is it? So what's the problem?' Tim said. 'We could have a quick run down the line tonight and nobody any the wiser.'

'How far'll we go?' Simon asked, wishing he'd thought of it first, wishing Tim didn't take everything over; he was too inclined to be bossy and to jump first and test the water afterwards, for Simon's more cautious approach to life.

Duggy polished his hair furiously—desperately—with a greasy hand, but he knew that it was no use protesting; besides—he had intended to have a surreptitious solo go on the railmotor. He did not, however, fancy taking the entire gang for a ride. There was bound to be trouble.

'Dad'll go mad,' he repeated. 'But OK. I'll drive the railmotor—but mind, just this once! It's a crime to trespass on railways—let alone drive on them.'

'Well, they'll hardly hang all of us—probably just you, Duggy. Remember, you're in charge, lad.' Tim sat down beside Cathy, combing his thick untidy fair hair out of his eyes with a grubby hand, peering at the controls.

'Can I come?' Cathy's voice and eyes were bland. 'That was my last question, by the way. And it was my idea. And we are all members of the Society. Hey, do you think we might get expelled from ALPS—if they find out, I mean?'

'Very likely, but I suppose you'd better come,' Duggy said grudgingly, adding under his breath: 'We'll get no peace otherwise.'

'Funny, isn't it, the way women manipulate us?' Tim said to nobody in particular. 'Must be an inborn thing, like being better at washing up and things like that . . . '

'You mean womanipulate,' Chas muttered.

Everybody groaned. It was going to be that sort of day.

'Right. Now—' Tim slid off the seat, leaned against the side of the railmotor and folded his arms. 'Haltwhistle and back—or bust.'

Duggy opened and shut his mouth; no sound emerged. He felt control slipping. What was he letting himself in for?

'It won't take long, will it?' Simon asked doubtfully. 'Only, you know what they're like . . . ' Everybody knew that 'they' referred to their collective parents.

'We can't drive right down to Haltwhistle, mind.' Duggy warned. 'It's about eight miles each way, so we'll stop before we get to Haltwhistle viaduct. If the railmotor does twenty miles an hour, that'll take us roughly—well—under an hour. The later we start the better—fewer folk about. Not before ten o'clock, anyway.' Once committed, he was keen to make the run a success.

'It'll be great!' Cathy exclaimed, suddenly wildly excited. 'Slipping silently down the midnight line, on silver wheels and silver track, on the very first run for years and years.' She jumped down and dusted her hands on the seat of her jeans. 'It'll be something to remember . . . '

Duggy felt it wasn't necessary to explain that the new track had been tested and approved before the Light Railway Order was granted. You didn't just stick a few miles of lines down and run a passenger railway without trying it first. Not to mention the locos and rolling stock—they had to be tested too. The Railway Inspectorate had overseen all that, apart from the 0–4–0 shunter at Slaggyford. He glanced over at it, all painted and polished, waiting for a boiler test. The house would seem bare without the 0–4–0 sitting next to the front room. He noticed that the fog had almost lifted. He was scarcely aware of a slight flash which seemed to come from Williamston Fell, on the opposite side of the valley, just above the mist; the back of his mind dismissed it as the sun glinting off—something. It wouldn't do any harm to let Cathy think this was a sort of maiden voyage—keep her happy. Sometimes it seemed important that Cathy should be happy. Funny, there was that flash again. Must be somebody—a hiker mebbe— over yonder.

'How can it be a midnight line at ten o'clock?' Chas was asking curiously.

'Don't be so— so—.' Cathy spluttered, glaring at him for spoiling her poetic fancy.

'Pedantic?' Solemnly Chas supplied the missing word.

'Poetic, that,' Tim considered, his head on one side. 'The Midnight Line . . .'

'Huh,' Duggy grunted. He was sick of Tim and Chas and their posh accent; you never knew if they were laughing at you, or with you, but he always suspected it was 'at'.

'Nothing poetic about railways.'

'Right. Then we'll grind noisily down the ten o'clock line,' Tim retorted.

'I'm just about sick of standing about listening to a lot of rubbish.' Duggy suddenly jumped up on to the platform. The others followed him into the waiting-room out of the damp.

'It's horrible now, after the fine morning.' Cathy shivered. She sat down next to Simon on the end of the LNER-green batten seat.

'Oh, ar!' Tim said. 'Fine afore seven, rain afore eleven.'

'What?' Cathy asked, bewildered.

'Shut it!' Simon said. 'I'm sick of listening to everybody wittering on about nothing.'

After a short silence, Cathy sniffed. She scuffed the toes of her shoes among the drift of last year's larch needles, which had blown in from the trees alongside the waiting-room.

Duggy glanced at his mates, sitting like crows on a dyke.

'It's not wet now. The sun was shining over yonder just now—fog's lifting. It's going to work, you know—the line, I mean. Lambley Viaduct was a bit dodgy, but it's been done up. Burnstone Viaduct's been sort of adopted by some society or other, 'cos it's unique—skew—'

'Look up—he's off again,' Simon groaned, gazing up at the ceiling. 'Our walking, talking railway enthusiast's encyclopaedia.'

'Really keen on this railway stuff, aren't you, Duggy?' Tim

was deliberately egging Duggy on to aggravate Simon still further. 'It'll be with your Dad and Grandad being engine-drivers. You've got it from them.'

'It's like Eton, you know,' Chas said, looking down at his feet so that his hair fell over his face.

Everybody stared at him.

'What is?' Cathy asked.

'Well—being a loco-driver. Steam. You have to put your name down at birth, to be one. Read it somewhere . . .'

'Precocious,' Tim said. 'Writing at birth . . .'

'What a wasted morning,' Simon complained. 'I thought we were going to go over the railmotor—we'd have been better off at home.'

'No, you wouldn't,' Cathy reminded him smartly. 'You would've had to work!'

'I've enjoyed my day so far,' Tim stretched his long legs luxuriously. 'And anyway, you can't do much when it's cold and damp.'

Cathy jumped to her feet.

'I'm starving!' she announced. 'Let's go down to the Post Office and get some apples or something.'

'Too late. Milly's just gone into her gate—must be dinnertime.' From his end seat, Simon could see down the station bank towards the village where the road divided, one branch bearing left past a few cottages, to the Post Office, which Milly, the postmistress, had locked up for the weekend, the other continuing down to meet the main A689 road.

'Saturday—it's half-day. I know, let's bike up to Alston—see what's going on—might get something to eat at the Station Café. We might get it cost price, with Duggy being on the staff and his Mum being part café-owner and chief cook.' Simon grinned, glad of the prospect of action. He was pleased Duggy had made it plain that he didn't want the Cubbys messing about with his railmotor. Clever, they were; mechanics they were not.

'And Chas and I'll catch the one o'clock bus up 'cos we haven't got our bikes.' Tim patted each of his pockets in turn. 'Have you any money on you, Chas?' he asked, turning to his twin.

'I have—but we'll walk part of the way to save hanging about for the bus for half an hour.' And Chas added: 'You can pay me back when we get home.'

Having parted with the Cubbys at the foot of Lintley Bank,and and then watched them waving from the rear window as the bus negotiated the first bend, Simon, Duggy and Cathy set off on their bicycles.

'Mind and keep right in to the left,' Simon called over his shoulder. 'There's an idiot coming down far too fast—look out!'

They struggled up the hill in single file, concentrating on keeping well in to the gravelly verge as a huge bread-delivery van came towards them, well over the central white line.

Seconds later they were overtaken and forced off the road like a row of skittles.

Simon was the first to pick himself up from the narrow verge. He glared after the vehicle which had come up from behind.

It was a red Range Rover.

The red Range Rover—the one with the non-matching driver.

3

Shakily, Cathy stooped to pick up her cycle, when she noticed that a ring of denim had been torn off the hem of one leg of her jeans and was hanging on the right pedal.

'Did you see that?' she said, suddenly furious. 'Did you see who it was? And look what he's done!' She stuffed the blue material into her pocket. 'You two OK?'

Cathy's face was white and pinched, and they were all more shaken than they would admit, but they climbed back on their cycles.

Simon found his voice—and his quick temper.

'That was the daftest trick I've ever seen. You can't credit it. Overtaking on this hill and right on a blind bend. That lunatic must've missed the bread-van by fractions of a second—they could've crashed head-on.'

'Serve them right if they had!' Duggy snarled. 'They deserved to crash—that's as near as I ever want to be to that perishing maniac. Like I said before—cars should be banned.'

Simon held up his arm in a rude gesture.

'It was him, wasn't it, Si? That chap that shouted at you outside the Post Office for breathing on his Rover the other day?' Duggy returned the gesture enthusiastically. It was wasted on Simon's back, but the driver of an approaching car looked puzzled.

'It was him OK—recognised the number-plates. He's still

running on trade plates. Funny, seeing him up here again—he's not local . . . But at least he'll be well away by now, the speed he was doing. And we're out of the mist now.'

Railway, road and river meandered up the valley, between the greening bracken and heather-clad fells. Pockets of snow still showed on Cross Fell, as if defying the approach of summer.

'Sometimes I think we're the only people still alive—we've hardly seen a living soul all day, not counting the Cubbys. It's creepy—as if everybody's been swallowed up in cars and houses, like your money used to be swallowed up in those vacuum things in that old-fashioned shop in Hexham—you know, just sucked away and never seen again. There's no sign of life at all !' Cathy panted. 'Only sheep !'

Simon recognised the signs. Cathy always talked a lot about nothing when she was upset. It seemed to help, and she didn't notice if nobody else joined in.

Without further incident they arrived at Brewery Bridge; as they crossed the South Tyne they saw that Alston was crowded with visitors. The garage and car-parks were full, the road lined with parked cars. They kept left, past the junction where the picturesque cobbled street began the steep climb to the Market Cross, almost a thousand feet above sea level.

'This is where everybody's got to—just look at all those cars and flags and banners.' Cathy pointed up the hill as they went past. 'Cars as far as you can see—must be hordes of visitors in already. Funny really, when you think—it's a new railway that's opening, not a motorway! Let's hope we can find Tim and Chas in the crush.'

They free-wheeled down to the station-yard gates and stopped under a banner which stretched overhead: GRAND OPENING: ALSTON LINE: MAY DAY.'

'We'll never find anybody in that crowd. Be easier if we hadn't bikes to cart about. Suppose we could put them over yonder, out of the way.' Simon waved towards the old foundry yard, opposite the station.

'No, we'll chuck them in Olive's front garden—she'll not mind. I'll take them,' Duggy offered. 'The dog knows me.'

They eased down the station-yard approach, then passed their cycles over the fence for Duggy to stow in the garden shed. Duggy kept a wary eye on the snappy Border terrier which bounded up as he opened the wicket gate; he closed it smartly.

'That dog has a short memory' Cathy pointed out, 'I thought it knew you.'

'Different dog,' Duggy said.

They then separated to look for the Cubbys.

Cathy squeezed among the crowds but finally gave up, spotted her brother leaning against the shop wall, and joined him.

'I hate and detest crowds!' she exclaimed, pulling a wry face.

'Me too, but you can't run a railway without 'em—or an antique shop.' Against his will Simon was impressed by the atmosphere and general excitement. He had not realised how many people were interested in the new line—and it wasn't even opening-day yet.

Cathy stood on tiptoe, watching people milling about the yard, which was separated from the station platform by the long row of buildings adjoining the house, with its high chimneys and gables and huge 'cannon-balls'. The shop was next to the house, then a high covered archway, and on the other side of the arch, which incorporated a ticket-office, lay the waiting-rooms and storage-rooms. A signpost pointed out the various attractions on the platform, including the observation coaches which stood at the buffers end of the station. Cathy noticed that most people made for the archway, squeezing through to reach the shop, café, and coaches and the museum, which was new to her. More rolling-stock would be on the sidings, north of the station, although she couldn't see anything because of the crowd.

She turned to try and peer through the back window of the shop, but there was a net curtain across it.

'Doesn't look as if we'll ever find anything to eat here,' she commented as Duggy joined them. Immediately she felt even more hungry. 'We might never get out of here alive. They've really gone to town with publicity and everything.'

Simon grabbed her arm. 'Look over yonder, between the wall of that warehouse and the back wall of the yard, below the Hexham road. See? The red Range Rover. Nobody's supposed to park there—it's private, no admittance except on business. But then, it's just what you'd expect from a moron like him—he probably can't read that "Private" sign.' He grinned. 'I want a word with that driver . . .'

Cathy hung back, not wanting to be involved, but feeling that she should support Simon.

'Come on!' Simon shouted impatiently over his shoulder, pushing against the tide of incomers streaming in from the main road. Duggy towed Cathy towards the Rover.

A tall, lean, alert-looking man, wearing a brown tweed suit, leaned against the red car, with his head through the open window, talking to two men in the back seat. His feet, Cathy noticed, were crossed at the ankles; his tan brogues looked expensive—and dirty. She saw, without really noticing, that he wore unsuitable, fine black socks. She wrinkled her nose in distaste. She couldn't have explained why, but she couldn't bear to see anybody standing with his ankles crossed.

'Just stick to the original—' he was saying. He broke off and half-turned as the three teenagers approached. Thick black hair flopped over his forehead; he shook it back impatiently, his dark eyes narrowing as, without apparent recognition, he watched them.

However . . . he had known when they started out for

Alston. He knew of Duggy's interest in the line and the Society. He had known their every movement over the previous week. He knew, in fact, more than was good for them.

'Well, and what do you kids want?'

Simon knew that voice; he had been shouted at by it, outside the Post Office. His mother would have called it 'put-on refined', although the language was anything but refined.

Surprisingly, it was Duggy who spoke first. He planted his feet apart and stuck his hands in his boiler-suit pockets; his grubby face and ears were red and shiny; he glowered.

'I'll tell you what we want—we want to know why you tried to run us down on Lintley Bank. You were driving like a drunken maniac—and I've a good mind to report you for dangerous driving.' Further infuriated by the driver's insolent expression, Duggy took a step nearer.

'And you overtook us on a blind corner,' Simon joined in. 'I know you can see further ahead in a Rover than you can in an ordinary car, but that was suicidal—we were cycling well into our side, but there isn't room to overtake there.'

'And you made us all fall off our bikes.' Cathy finished indignantly. 'Look—my jeans are torn—and my ankle's bruised, and it's all your fault.' As she spoke Cathy discovered that her ankle was indeed sore. She leaned down to massage it, and noticed that her ALPS badge-pin was unfastened. She pinned the green and silver membership badge firmly on to her anorak.

The driver, completely ignoring their outburst, turned away and resumed his conversation in what seemed like an even more exaggerated accent.

'Aren't you coming to see what's on offer in Alston, before you put on your rucksacks? We shall have to find somewhere to eat—that is, if there's anything more ambitious than a fish-and-chip shop in this benighted place.'

This time it was Simon who stepped forward and said, quietly and distinctly: 'Don't try any of the hotels or cafés here —they don't encourage riff-raff. There's a doss-house in Newcastle. They might take you in, if they're not too fussy—and it's far enough from here not to matter to us . . . '

The stranger's face seemed to puff out; his neck reddened, but with an obvious effort he swallowed the insult and said nothing. His companions stepped down from the Range Rover; they wore crumpled, washed-out khaki jeans and combat jackets, and walking boots with thick fawn stockings turned down over their tops. First lifting down three framed rucksacks, they closed the Rover's windows and doors, then all three men faced Simon.

The second one had stubby ginger hair and white eyelashes and a matching set of thick eyebrows which almost met over his light blue eyes. His pallid face was freckled—even his all-but-lobeless ears had a sprinkling of pale freckles. The third man was slight and small; quite insignificant, except for dark blue eyes fringed by thick, straight black lashes. His dark short hair was cut level all the way round his small, round head.

Suddenly fear touched Cathy, Simon and Duggy as they recognised the cold menace in the three pairs of eyes. They felt vulnerable, even though people were milling about only a few yards away. Cathy knew she would never forget the expression in their eyes.

For the first time she felt that somebody hated her: in triplicate. It was a nasty feeling.

'Blasted kids—clear off before I flatten yis out,' snarled Ginger, but his companions gave him a warning look before they veered off to march diagonally across the station yard in the direction of the sidings, north of the buildings. Then Ginger turned and said menacingly: 'Don't forget—keep out of our road, else yis'll get hurt. And don't try anything on, else it'll be the worse for yis!' Then he ran to join the others, matching his step to theirs, shuffling his feet like an out-of-step soldier.

Simon and Duggy stared after them, then exchanged significant glances.

'Irish,' Duggy said. 'Wonder what the other one is—he never spoke.'

'If he's a Scot they'll be able to tell each other funny stories.' Cathy gave a relieved laugh, as if making a joke about the incident would lessen the tension; nobody else laughed.

'What was all that about?'

They looked round as they heard a familiar amused voice. Tim was bearing down on them, taller than most of the crowd and balancing promising-looking greaseproof-paper bags in either hand, held high above his head, like a couple of trays.

'Bacon sandwiches,' he explained. 'Personalised by Duggy's mum—she hid these in the fridge in case we turned up. It's chaos in that café ! It's OK, Cathy—we heated them up. And you didn't mention that your mum was going to be here full-time, Duggy—she's flying about like a paper kite in a gale o'wind in yonder.'

Equally tall but only half as wide as Tim, Chas followed, holding five paper cups of soup by their handle, his bony wrists, as usual, four inches longer than his sleeves.

'You're a couple of geniuses,' Cathy mumbled, nibbling round the edges of a sandwich.

'Mm—we know,' Tim agreed modestly.

Simon finished his meal first, then explained to Tim and Chas what had happened in their absence.

'Sounds a bit sinister to me,' Tim said, raking lentils from the bottom of his cup with a crooked forefinger, and eyeing Duggy at the same time. 'But then, you get a lot of cranks interested in railways . . . bound to be a lot of 'em here this weekend . . . .'

'I'm sick of Alston.' Cathy announced. 'Those men've put me right off. There's nothing we can do here. All the ALPS members seem to have turned up to help, judging by the hundreds of people I've noticed wearing little green and silver badges in their lapels.' She patted her own badge, checking that it was securely fastened. 'Why did we come here, anyway?'

'Food, dear. And it was your idea, was it not? But we haven't seen the posh coaches yet—you can't get near them for cameras and reporters.'

Tim crumpled their cups.

'I know,' Duggy declared, watching Tim. 'Let's go and take a look at the Daler. I think she'll be in that shed over yonder—prob'ly locked—but Dad's bound to be about somewhere. He'll have kittens if anybody lays a finger on that loco. He'll be watching over it like a hawk . . . Funny, though —our car's not in its usual place.'

Simon yawned, but the old restored loco had had a lot of publicity and he was more interested than he appeared to be. Duggy was determined to show off what he considered to be his family's private railway, and its famous Daler.

'Oh, all right! We'll go and investigate,' Simon agreed with a show of reluctance. 'But don't go on about it, there's a good lad . . . Cars and tractors are more in my line . . . By the way Tim, you seem very attached to that bag of rubbish.' Then he grinned. 'Give it here – might as well do something useful with it . . . '

He compacted the bag of paper cups into a cylinder roughly the diameter of a Rover exhaust pipe . . . He thought fleetingly that this was the sort of silly trick Tim usually thought of first.

'Tut tut,' Tim said, wagging a forefinger at Simon. 'You should be ashamed of yourself. Vandalising that nice man's Range Rover . . . You know, Si, you are growing into the sort of person your mother wouldn't want you to associate with.'

Still grinning, Simon edged behind the warehouse and neatly fitted the cylinder into the Rover's exhaust pipe, while Tim kept a look-out. Then all five made their way over the yard to the sheds. They stumbled over the piles of unidenti- fiable, useful things which are generally to be found lying about the perimeters of preserved railways, and arrived at the north end, fully expecting Duggy's parent to be on guard round the closed sheds, on the sidings, or in the open-ended shed.

'Everything's locked up, and no sign of Big Duggy,' Cathy said, disappointed.

Duggy was both puzzled and worried as he ran to recheck the sheds. But all were bolted, barred and padlocked.

'Look,' Cathy whispered, pointing to a sign fastened to the high, heavy link-fencing between the sheds and the road beyond. 'This site is guarded by closed-circuit television,' it read.

'Well, it'll have to be protected I suppose – the Daler will be worth quite a bit; they'll not want to risk souvenir-hunters stripping it down. Like piranhas, some of them,' Tim said.

'The gauge-glass covers disappeared from the engine at Slaggyford,' Duggy said, 'And the pressure gauge and windows were smashed. We should have covered the whole loco in sticky grease, that might have kept their thieving hands off.'

'You'd have thought there would be something going on here – maintenance and all that stuff.' Simon spoke slowly, not wanting to mention Unicus, which, he reckoned, would be stabled here, ready for Monday. It was up to Duggy to tell Tim and Chas about his dad's new loco if and when he wanted to.

But there was no sound from inside the sheds.

Duggy wondered bleakly where his Dad had got to . . . He

had promised Duggy an illicit private preview of Unicus, as well as the Daler, yet here he was—gone.

Silently and with one accord, the five wandered down the sidings, away from the now muted hum of the station, past an enamelled sign bearing the warning: 'It is dangerous to go beyond this sign.'

Seeing but not noticing the lines of fairly modern rolling-stock, they continued beyond the lever frame and points to the river bridge carrying the track north to Haltwhistle.

They leaned over the parapet and watched a dipper fishing from a half-submerged rock in the middle of the South Tyne.

'I've pro'bly mentioned this before, but some days I wake up all sort of jangly inside—you know? And I know that something's going to go wrong—and it usually does.' Cathy spoke slowly, gazing down at the small black and white bird as it dived repeatedly into the fast-flowing brown river. 'This morning I felt jangly. That's why I can't sort of settle to do anything, and I don't think we should go on the railmotor tonight.'

'Pathetic!' Tim jerked upright and turned round to lean against the bridge, his elbows resting on the rough capestones. 'We're going to be the first down the line if it's the last thing we do.' He stared curiously at Cathy. 'Anyway, I hadn't got you down as pathetic . . . '

'Don't talk wet,' Simon snapped, referring to his sister. His eyebrows were set at stormy. 'Course we're going—what can go wrong?'

'Anyway,' Duggy put in accusingly, 'it was your idea in the first place! But I've got to find out about Dad first . . . '

'Well, it's different now. I've changed my mind—and I can't forget the way those men looked at us . . . ' Cathy shivered.

Chas looked from one to the other and began to hum.

4

The previous weekend a man dressed in brilliantly obvious country clothes—thornproof tweeds, Barbour jacket and walking boots, all new and as yet untouched by thorns, rain or mud—had parked his car in a lay-by at Eals bridge, and, having first checked that his fishing-rod, bait box and current copy of *Sporting Life* could be seen on the back seat by any passers-by, shouldered a laden rucksack and binoculars before setting off walking, rather stiffly, up a steep track at the north-eastern end of the bridge. He crossed the shoulder of Williamston Common at a thousand feet, reached the shelter of a derelict farmhouse marked Stokeld Green on his map, and laid his rucksack on what had been the kitchen floor. The flagstones were broken now, indistinguishable from the surrounding stony fell land.

Immediately he went outside and climbed higher up the fell, stumbling over hidden rocks and dead heather roots; turning frequently to scan the village opposite, until, well satisfied, he nodded and raised his binoculars. From this height he was able to see the buildings on the Tate and Cubby farms, most of Burnhaugh farm track, and all of the tarmac road which dropped down sharply to the station and the village.

Little that happened in this part of the South Tyne valley during the next week escaped him. He noted in minute detail what went on in Knarsdale Parish: the times of buses, postman and milkman, butcher and fishmonger; who went out to work and who did not. He noted particularly the movements of the Stevens family; saw the huffy parting between Duggy and the young Tates at the station-house door and the subsequent reconciliation; and noted the advent of the Cubby twins.

He wished he had learned to lip-read . . . .

Duggy's green tank-engine, standing north of the station house, concealed the railmotor from his view, but on the Saturday he saw the five young folk walk down to the main road, three of them pushing bikes, until the fog hid them, then he saw the top of the red bus when it stopped to pick up the Cubbys. He smiled briefly as a Range Rover—also red—skimmed past the cyclists as they emerged from the low bank of fog.

He nodded to himself as he put down his radio-telephone. Everything seemed to be going to plan. He hoped that his own small private plan would go as well . . . .

5

After much discussion it was decided that they should search the buildings again for any sign of Big Duggy before making for home. There was nothing to be gained by staying at Alston now that any chance of inspecting the locos had receded. The crowded station seemed strange now, as if it no longer belonged to them—as if it had turned its back on them.

A thorough search revealed no more than a couple of small boys chugging along the track, pretending to be trains; of Big Duggy there was no sign.

'Tell you what,' Tim looked from Duggy to Simon to Cathy. 'Chas and I are without bike, so to speak, so we'll walk home along the railway track, 'cos it's a mile shorter than the road. You three could bike along that back road yonder.' He nodded towards the high fence behind the Range Rover, beyond which the unclassified road on the east side of the river ran to join the A689 at Slaggyford. 'Bit bumpy, and there's gates and cattle-grids and probably the odd tiger, but at least you're not likely to meet that idiot again,' he pointed at the Rover. 'It's much quieter than the main Lintley Bank road.' Privately, he thought that Cathy would be a bit nervous of cycling back down the road they had had their narrow escape on. He was right.

Having arranged to meet the others at Duggy's house, Tim and Chas set off down the line, stepping awkwardly at first from sleeper to sleeper, then more briskly as they moved on to the newly ballast-strewn line-side. Neither of them noticed the old mud-spattered Land Rover and trailer parked at the road crossing near the disused Linger lime-loading dock. After all, old Land Rovers are part of the North Pennine scene. . . .

Tim and Chas were also unaware of two men standing behind the Land Rover, each carring a large, open, strong, plastic sack: waiting.

Few people noticed the sleek black Jaguar leaving Alston station and speeding past the Land Rover and trailer on the A686 road, slowing slightly to take the right-hand fork, instantly picking up speed on the hill.

A tall dark man in tweeds and dirty brogues parked the Jaguar outside Hexham police station and walked smartly into the reception area, where he asked the desk sergeant to investigate the theft of a friend's new Range Rover from outside a garage in Hexham.

'Can't miss it!' he said in a hearty voice. 'Still has its trade plates up—bright red—quite ostentatious, really.' And he handed the sergeant a card all neatly typed with a fictitious telephone number and address in York.

Well pleased, he exchanged nods with a policeman entering the station, returned to his car and drove sedately half a mile out of Hexham to a secluded farmhouse whose occupants appeared to be moving out. A large articulated trailer and unit was parked in the yard, with its ramp lowered.

The black Jaguar eased up the ramp and disappeared inside the trailer.

A few minutes later a middle-aged man emerged, wearing jeans, anorak and the obligatory woolly hat. He adjusted his rucksack, tucked a stray strand of hair inside the blue knitted hat and strode off briskly—for a middle-aged man—towards the station to catch the 16.12 train to Haltwhistle.

Cathy, Simon and a glum-seeming Duggy cycled along the riverside road as far as the tiny Kirkhaugh Church, when Cathy braked suddenly.

'It's my ankle. Must've grazed it when that oaf made us all fall off our bikes It's bleeding a bit—look. . . .'

'How come you haven't noticed it till now?' Simon sounded unsympathetic as he stared critically at Cathy's ankle. 'Tim could've taken your bike and you could've caught a bus home if you'd said . . . There's not much traffic on this road—how d'ye think you're going to get a lift?'

Cathy glared at him.

'I don't want a lift! It's fine when I walk. But the pedal catches it, so I'll just walk home and push my bike. It'll not be the first time, and I can free-wheel on the down bits—I'll be OK.'

'Well, if you're sure,' Simon sounded uncertain but he was, Cathy knew, furious with her, because he would feel responsible for her and she had mucked up his plans. He went on: 'But for Pete's sake mind what you're doing and don't take lifts from anybody we don't know . . . '

But Cathy had already moved off, giggling because Simon sounded just like their Mum, and limping because her ankle really was sore.

Duggy and Simon waved as they cycled past her.

'You never know how to take them, do you?' Simon remarked to a bewildered Duggy.

'Who?'

'Lasses!'

Cathy was not so sure of being all right, once she was on her own on the road, with the prospect of a long climb up to the junction with the Ayle road. Her ankle was smarting; she wished she didn't have to keep asserting her independence. She usually came off worse in the end, but she couldn't bear being condescended to.

She stopped and looked about. The old rectory, the tiny, tall-spired Kirkhaugh church, the farm buildings: all were deserted, sunk in Saturday-afternoon gloom. Although she was accustomed to solitude—to living on a remote farm—Cathy felt apprehensive about the long walk home. She could have asked Simon to walk with her. He wouldn't have minded much, though he would have felt obliged to make a fuss. She was surrounded by fells, rising fold upon fold to the horizon. A few sheep and cattle moved about in search of new spring growth. Peewits and curlews called and wheeled about the sky. Along the haughs, by the gravelly riverside, a colony of oyster-catchers piped; she loved to watch them flying up the river to their nesting place, from their winter feeding ground on the Solway coast. Ahead, the road took a right-hand bend then went steeply uphill to the T-junction.

Still, no use looking at the hill; once at the top and through the farm gate she could coast along the side of the fell, and up on top it wouldn't be so claustrophobic.

Cathy set her shoulders, lifted her chin and started walking; after a while she cycled until her ankle hurt again, then walked. Half-way up the hill she heard the distinctive note of a Land Rover engine and a few seconds later the Land Rover overtook her and stopped, the tyres squealing.

'Hurray!' she thought. 'Somebody I know—Dad, mebbe, or the Robsons.'

Then she remembered that her parents would be busy ferrying china up to the shop; the Robsons, who were the only farmers on this side of the river between Kirkhaugh and

Slaggyford, were at a farm sale today. The few former farmhouses on this road belonged to weekenders—incomers: pleasant and helpful, but definitely not Land Rover bike-lift material.

The Land Rover completely blocked the narrow road. The ratchet grated as the driver pulled on the hand-brake. Simon would have cringed at the sound, she thought; he would have pretended to look underneath for teeth shearing off the quadrant . . .

She did not recognise the Land Rover.

Her heart quivered then sank; no chance of a lift. You had to be sure about who you took lifts from.

Then: 'Want a lift?' a rough voice asked. 'Slaggyford, isn't it? Your bike'll go in the trailer . . . . I'll put it in for yis . . . ' He opened the nearside door and jumped down, plumply.

Petrified, Cathy recognised the ginger man; he obviously recognised her . . . She wondered why he had swapped the Range Rover for this older vehicle. And where were the other men—were they here too?

She turned to go back down the hill, planning desperately how to escape. If she cycled down to the church and cut over the field and across the foot-bridge over the Tyne—joined the Lintley road at the top of the fields—they couldn't follow her there, even in a Land Rover. The Tyne was too deep to ford; the ginger man too fat to run as fast as she could, sore ankle and all . . .

But the small dark man—the driver—had got out and was waiting behind her, not exactly threatening; more—inevitable.

He held a large black sack in his hands.

'Don't struggle now and you'll be all right.' His voice was as soft as the ginger man's was harsh. 'Just keep quiet and you won't be harmed.'

Trapped, Cathy hung on to her bicycle. Ginger prised her fingers off the handle-bars. Cathy kicked at his ankles, but her training shoes made little impression on his thick socks and boots.

Ginger put her cycle in the trailer. Cathy pushed her trembling hands into her pockets and flexed her stomach muscles.

'Must'nt let them see I'm scared,' she told herself. The denim patch torn from her jeans was in the right-hand pocket; she pulled it out in the palm of her hand and let it slide down to the ground. Somebody might notice it and wonder, she thought bleakly. Then the sack slithered over her head and shoulders and down to her feet.

She kicked and struggled, but she knew it was no use. A

rope tightened round her ankles so that she overbalanced and was lifted into the back of the Land Rover and placed neatly alongside two similar sacks, although she did not know this at the time.

Humiliated and ashamed of not trying to escape until too late, Cathy lay, dazed and only vaguely aware of the Land Rover revving hard, turning sharp right at the top of the hill, and on to a bumpy track.

In the front seat, Ginger and the driver exchanged thumbs-up signs.

'Three down, two to go,' the driver said.

The Land Rover travelled along the Ayle road for a mile or so and stopped beside a plantation of dark fir trees. Ginger slid between the closely-growing trees and reappeared carrying a green metal box—almost the size and shape of a trunk. He loaded it into the trailer; three more boxes were added, then Ginger climbed back into his seat.

With a significant nod to the driver, Ginger relaxed, shuffling in his seat, while the Land Rover reversed and returned to the junction and followed the route taken by Simon and Duggy after they had parted from Cathy.

'Right oh,' Ginger said. 'OK for time so far, but we've still got to find the other two yins—can't have got far, though. We'll soon pick them up.' He scanned the road ahead through the dead-fly-stippled windscreen. 'Why did they separate like that? Still, you've got to be prepared for kids being like that.'

But they reached Barhaugh without seeing the two remaining cyclists.

'They can't have got this far—it's not possible,' Lee, the driver, said, frowning. 'Four miles in under ten minutes—nobody can cycle that fast on this road. They would have to walk up that steep hill, like the girl did. It's impossible for us to have missed them—there is no other way. Besides, Sven will be keeping an eye out for them. He would let us know if anything untoward happened. They must have stopped for a rest—we'll find them on the way back. We'll turn in this gateway just here—and we'll have to step on it. Max's train is due at Haltwhistle at 4.32 and we've got to dump the kids first, then meet the train—check with Max.'

'They're going to muck things up if we don't find them,' Ginger commented, glancing quickly at Lee's grim face, then back to the road. 'Why the blazes did they part company? Must have had a row or something.'

'We'll find them OK,' said Lee more confidently. 'After all, we've got this valley sewn up. Sven will be watching anything that moves, from that eyrie of his—though how he can live in that hovel for days on end I do not know. We'll have to contact him on the RT if we don't find the kids.'

'We shouldn't use the radio yet in case somebody picks us up. You never know who could be listening in and there'll be hell to pay if we fumble this one!'

Ginger's Irish accent was more pronounced now.

'Everything seems quiet enough—I mean, why should anybody suspect anything when nothing's happened so far?' But in spite of seeming cheerful, Lee's brows were still creased in a V.

They did not find Simon and Duggy on the road to Slaggyford.

6

Having left Cathy trudging along, Simon and Duggy struggled up the bank to the T-junction, standing on their pedals in spite of Lee's expectations. They turned left, opened a gate which bore the painted-on advice to 'shut yet', and were on a relatively level stretch. They bent over their handlebars and pedalled fast, past a derelict farmhouse with mullion and transom windows, a new cottage and sheep pens. Then Simon's front wheel found a tramline crack in the road surface and stopped. His rear wheel kept going and tipped Simon over the handlebars on to the grass verge.

Duggy swerved to avoid the crack, wobbled and overbalanced.

'Heck me!' he roared, picking himself up. 'You OK, Si?'

'Think so,' Simon stood up cautiously, flexing all movable parts. 'You know, I was looking forward to a nice quiet ride home . . . '

'Me too. Oh, come on Si, we'll go back by the railway. We can hang about for a bit till Tim and Chas turn up, then walk the rest of the way with them—they can't have got far—I don't think they'll have passed us yet.'

'Right,' Simon agreed. 'At least it'll be better than falling off our bikes every five minutes—I mean—that's twice today. Mind you, I didn't realise the road was so bad, and then all those gates to open.'

They turned off the road, down the fields towards the river.

'Wonder how far your Cathy's got—no sign of her yet. We'll have to keep out of her sight or she'll want to come as well, but the railway'll be too rough a walk for her sore ankle,' Duggy said, glancing at Simon, who only grunted.

They negotiated the grassy track through the next field at the bottom of the hill and crossed the narrow, blue-painted foot-bridge over the river.

'Lucky it happened near here—this is the only bridge over the South Tyne between Alston and Slaggyford,' Duggy panted, heaving his cycle over the railway fence. 'It's not one of our better days though, is it?' He rubbed an even grubbier than usual hand over his hair, waiting for Simon to join him.

'Mm, they seem to come in cycles,' Simon said, straight-faced. 'But the railmotor trip later on'll make up for all this, eh? We'll just wait here for a few minutes till the Cubbys show up.'

So, unaware that Cathy was even then starting up the hill down which they had just scrambled, Simon and Duggy waited for Tim and Chas, grew tired of hanging about, and dawdled along the ballast by the trackside, in a tree-tunnel which effectively hid them from view. They were unaware that Cathy was only seconds away from being kidnapped, and that Tim and Chas had already been kidnapped.

Although they walked a slow to moderate pace, retracing their steps more than once, Simon and Duggy reached Slaggyford level crossing without seeing Tim and Chas.

And when Cathy failed to show up within a reasonable time, Simon voiced the worry which had gnawed away at the back of his mind all afternoon, although he had tried not to show it, to avoid adding to Duggy's apprehension.

'It takes no more than an hour and a half to walk the full distance from Alston—she should've been back by now, even allowing an hour extra for having to push her bike.' He looked at Duggy gloomily.

'Well, it's not like Cathy not to show up—but you never seem to know with lasses. She could have met some of her cronies and gone off with them.'

'But Cathy just wouldn't do that!' Simon spoke vehemently; the thought had crossed his mind, but he felt guilty at having left his sister and thought that a bit of loyalty wouldn't come amiss. 'And besides, it's Saturday, remember. There's never anybody about here on a Saturday—most of Cath's friends go shopping, or to work. But none of them hang about here—' he waved his arm at the deserted platform. 'Next week, now, when your trains are running—things should be a bit more lively then.'

Duggy looked bleak at the mention of trains, remembering what had happened at Alston, remembering his Dad's absence, but he replied cheerfully enough: 'Right enough, Si. I'm glad you've come round to my way of thinking about the line being a good thing . . . But what about Tim and Chas? We never saw hair nor hide of them on the railway—and we should have. I mean, they can't have got here before us—and they can't have got a lift either. So where are they? Where is everybody?'

'Duggy, they could have walked by the Pennine Way!' Simon exclaimed then thought again. 'No, mebbe not. We'd have seen them, surely.'

With a heavy sinking feeling, Simon realised that Cathy was somehow lost. He knew that she would never have gone on down to Lambley, or anywhere else, without a word to anybody. If he went up home to Burnhaugh on the off chance that she had gone there, and she hadn't, there would be one heck of a row. Forgetting that his parents were not at home, he imagined his Dad's eyes, black with anger; his Mum, white-faced and reproachful. If only Cathy had mentioned her sore ankle beforehand . . . If only those cretins hadn't run them down on Lintley Bank. But it all boiled down to the fact that it was his fault; he shouldn't have left her on her own. Tim and Chas would be OK—at least there were two of them. When they do turn up, he told himself savagely, I'll not half give them something to think about . . . wasting time for nothing when they should all be searching for Cathy.

'Then there's Dad's car—that's what's worrying me. Dad's missing as well,' Duggy said quietly. 'Everybody seems to be missing.'

Finally, as dusk approached, Simon suggested phoning the police.

'We don't want to worry anybody else—the police'll send a car to search for them. They'll know what to do,' he said dismally, knowing that they had already searched as well as anybody could. 'It's no use leaving it any longer, else it'll be too dark to see. Something must have happened.'

'Tell you what, Si, we'll go into my place and phone Mum at Alston—the café'll not be as busy now. She'll not mind. She'll know what to do—and we'll feel better if a grown-up knows about it.' Duggy led the way into the station-house back door, first fumbling behind a loose stone next to the door frame to find the key. He switched on the light.

The room was devastated.

7

Contents of the kitchen cupboards and drawers were heaped on the floor. Everything which could be ripped open was ripped open: cushions, chair seats, bags of flour, sugar.

Simon and Duggy stared in disbelief.

At last Simon spoke: 'Well, at least we know now that we have something to worry about.' He collapsed on to one of the mangled chairs, glanced obliquely at Duggy and asked: 'Dug—I mean, it's none of my business—but, well, does your Mum keep much money in the house? Will they have pinched very much? Not that it matters—it's the fact that somebody's actually turned over your private things. I mean the money matters but . . . ' he trailed miserably to a halt and stared at the floor.

Suddenly Duggy turned and rushed into the living-room, glanced at the mess in there and ran on, into the small sitting-room across the hall. Mystified, Simon followed, noting that all the doors were open. Mrs. Stevens always kept them shut, 'to keep the heat in' or 'in case of fire'.

Simon had never been in this, Mr Stevens's special room.

Rolls of blueprint paper were flung about; the drawing-board was tipped over, its stand shattered; books and papers were strewn everywhere. An old station clock lay on the floor, still ticking. The overhead light glanced off a collection of magnificent brass loco name-plates which covered one wall. Four quarter-mile posts supported the mantlepiece, which looked suspiciously like a planed and polished sleeper. Simon stared, fascinated.

Brass gauges and bridge number-plates decorated the fireplace wall; a long-bladed shovel stood in an upturned brass dome beside the cast-iron fireplace. A length of fish-bellied rail line lay along the front of a shelf crammed with railway books and magazines, above which were hung water-colours of Whitley Bay and Scarborough, painted in that unmistakable early railway style.

Intrigued in spite of himself, Simon grinned. Then to his horror he felt a bubble of laughter rising inside and he could do nothing about it. He began to shake with uncontrollable hysteria.

Duggy glared at him for a moment, then took hold of Simon's shoulders and shook him like a terrier with a rat, shouting: 'Shut up! Shut up! Stop it! Stop it, will you . . . ' Then, worn out, they collapsed into one of the plush-covered railway-carriage seats drawn up in front of the fireplace.

White-faced now, they avoided each other's eyes, then Simon spoke, awkwardly: 'Look, Duggy, I'm sorry—it's just that everything seemed to come together and hit me. I mean,I wasn't laughing at anything in particular—you know what I mean? Can't explain really . . . '

Duggy nodded, polishing his hair vigorously.

'And I didn't really want to knock your head off—I want to knock the head off whoever did all this.'

'We'll have to phone the police now—but what d'ye suppose the burglars were after? You'd think they'd have pinched some of those brass name-plates—must be worth a small fortune . . . Unless it was drunks that broke in.' Simon's voice sounded unconvincing even to himself.

'Naa. They would be after Dad's blueprints—for Unicus, you remember, his new loco. But they'll not have found them. He has them in a strong-box in the bank at Alston—both the

working drawings and the specifications,' Duggy explained.
Then his expression darkened and he added wearily: 'But you
know Dad—always changing, improving things. He'll have
another set of plans somewhere here.' He managed a feeble
grin, but his eyes were bleak. 'He hasn't a lot of patience for
paperwork. He's more for getting on with the job, but there's
the patents to think about. There was a man here a few days
ago—dunno who he was, but he was in here, and it's not
everybody that's allowed in this room, not even Mum when
Dad's working, 'cos she will keep tidying things away.' Duggy
lowered his voice. 'You see—well, a lot of stuff is er— Well,
strictly speaking we're not supposed to have it.' he ended in a
rush and his face turned bright red.

'You don't mean to say that your Dad's pinched all this
stuff?' Simon asked incredulously.

'No!' Duggy turned an indignant face towards Simon, but
he didn't meet his eyes. 'Well, not really—some of it, I
s'ppose. But mind, it was only to save it from being pinched
by other folk. Collectors pay a lot for this stuff, and Dad thinks
it belongs here, and not in a shop somewhere where they
don't understand about anything but money . . . I'm not
allowed in, really, but I sometimes come in when I'm on my
own.'

'So that's why——' Simon began, then stopped himself in
time from adding: 'your Mum keeps the door shut.' Instead
he said: 'So that's why you didn't sound too keen on phoning
the law. But we'll have to do something soon . . . Duggy! You
don't suppose that Cathy noticed somebody breaking in here
and tried to stop them?'

Duggy shook his head. 'Cathy wasn't here, man. Whoever it
was hasn't been long gone. This light was still on—and this
room hasn't been turned over as much as the other two.'

'Or else we disturbed him! Duggy, he could be still in the
house!'

They stared at each other apprehensively. Then the phone rang and they both jumped.

Duggy ran into the hall to answer it and came back looking puzzled.

'That was Cathy's friend from Lambley—you know, the one with the funny name: Melly or something. Anyway, she says that she was walking her dog along from Lambley station, just before tea, and the dog picked up something that she's sure belongs to Cathy: a handlebar grip. Melly remembers it because the grip split in half only last week, when Cathy was down at her place, and they mended it with Christmas Sellotape—red, she said it was, with green fir trees. She says to tell Cathy that she has it safe at home. She tried to phone Burnhaugh, but there was no reply.' He rubbed his hair and, avoiding Simon's surprised eyes, said: 'Er, Si, would you mind popping upstairs just in case the—the burglar's still in the house?'

Puzzled at Duggy's apparent nervousness, Simon dashed up the stairs three at a time, looked into the two bedrooms and bathroom and came straight back down.

Meanwhile, Duggy had pulled a model of Green Arrow from under the bookshelves, unscrewed the boiler front, pulled out a tube of stiff blue paper, refitted the boiler front, and replaced the loco before Simon reappeared. Only then did he let out a 'Phew' of relief.

Duggy waved the roll at Simon.

'Had an idea where this would be . . . Better if you didn't know. I'll post this on to the bank. It'll be safer there if we're going to be burgled for it. It's the blueprint, you know. Mum'll take a fit when she sees this mess!'

He went into the kitchen, picked up a roll of cooking-foil from the floor, unwound the foil, and slid the plan inside the cylinder of cardboard while Simon watched, open-mouthed at the quiet Duggy's grasp of the situation. Back in the sitting-room, Duggy found a pen and wrote the bank's address on the cylinder.

'You'll not get that in the post-box. Drop it in to Millie's. She'll post it for you on Monday—no, Tuesday. This is holiday Monday.' Simon spoke absently, wishing Duggy would get a move on and phone Mrs. Stevens.

'Imelda,' he said. 'That's Cath's friend's name. And I've just remembered seeing the handlebar grip! It was when Cathy complained about her ankle. I saw the tape then, so it was on her bike this afternoon! So how's it got to Lambley? Whereabouts did Melly find it? Did she say?'

Carefully, Duggy drew a line under the address, not looking up as he replied: 'Cinder path—you know, between the two brick houses and the station.'

Suddenly Simon was furious.

'The Cubbys and Cath—the lot of them must have gone down to Lambley somehow. . . Come on, Duggy!' Simon grabbed Duggy's arm. Then the phone rang again. They both went into the hall.

Simon watched Duggy pick up the receiver and almost immediately put it down.

'That was Dad.' Duggy stared down at the phone, rubbing his hair round absent-mindedly. 'He hung up before I could say anything! All he said was: "Everything's all right—don't worry and be sure to go up to old Duggy's—that's Grandad's—at Alston on Sunday night." That's all he said!'

'Well, that's something! At least we know your Dad's OK—and the plans are safe. All we've got to do is find Cathy and the Cubbys and give them a talking-to. And then there's the burglar . . .'

Duggy, knowing Big Duggy to be safe, was cheerful; he scribbled a note for Millie, the postmistress.

'There—we'll shove this in Millie's porch with the plans. Nobody'll think of looking there.' He glanced round the room. 'You don't think we should tidy up a bit?' he asked uneasily.

'For Pete's sake, come on, man—your Mum and you would've wanted to tidy the *Titanic*. By the way, I noticed the cellar door isn't bolted. Your Mum must have forgotten to do it.'

'You bolt it, Si, while I take a look round the back—in case anybody's lurking. But it doesn't feel as if anybody's watching—you can usually tell . . . .'

'Funny, us not noticing the light on in the front room—but then the shutters are closed . . . And the back door was locked! Duggy—how did the burglar get in? It just struck me that you unlocked the door—and there are no open or broken windows. And the front door's bolted, isn't it? Ours is never opened either . . . and you can't open a bolt from outside—so how could anybody get in?'

'I was wondering about that. I suppose he could've seen one of us taking the key from behind the loose stone outside the back door. It's a daft trick, that, leaving it there—but it's handy if you forget to take a key . . . He could have got in, turned the place upside down, got as far as Dad's room, heard us coming up the bank earlier on and got out round the front of the house. We couldn't have seen him—it's easy enough to slip round the side where the loco is without being seen from the road.'

'Aye well—however he got in, it'll mebbe teach you not to leave keys in safe places. I say, Duggy—it's funny, isn't it—a few minutes ago we were worried sick—and now things don't seem so bad. It's funny how ordinary things go on outside you, while inside you're sort of cringing with worry.'

8

Unaware that they were being closely observed by the hidden watcher on Williamston fell, Slaggyford villagers went about filling in their Saturday morning.

Having watched the arrival and departure of postman and milkman, the embarkation of Duggy's mother on the 9.42 bus to Alston, and the activities of the Tates, Cubbys and Stevens, Sven slotted his binoculars into their case, hitched on his ready-packed rucksack and came down the fell track with the fast-dispersing mist.

Once through Williamston farmyard and across the river bridge, he walked unhurriedly up the station bank and fetched up at the station-house. He knew where to find the key, having watched the Stevens's performance with the loose stone, but he did not need it, having previously—some six months previously—borrowed it and had a spare key cut before replacing it. Quickly now, he opened the door, went in, locked the door and pocketed his key.

Sven spent an entertaining but so far unproductive afternoon, turning out the kitchen and living room, and had just started on the sitting-room, when he heard voices outside, followed by the sound of the back door opening.

Something had gone wrong.

All of the kids should have been out of the way by now—tucked up in Lambley station shed. He had seen them setting off for Alston. He had radioed Lee to look out for them. Lee had checked and reported their every move. 'Birds moving upstream' he had said. He relaxed slightly; the intruders were not necessarily 'his' teenagers. The Stevenses probably had unexpected visitors. They would go away when nobody answered their call . . . They were noisy.

He moved out of the sitting-room and into the hall, leaving the light on in case it was visible from the outside; switching it off might draw attention to it..

After all, he reasoned, when the Lestrange outfit planned anything—in this case including the kidnapping of five kids—they would let nothing stop them. Had he ever known Ginger, Max, Lee, Jack—or any of the others—fail in anything they had undertaken over the past six years? No, he had not.

The fact that he was the intruder bothered him not at all. He had had enough of sitting in that draughty ruin on the fells; he had done what Lestrange wanted; now he was doing what he himself wanted: taking the blueprints of a revolutionary new loco—and, even more interesting, the material it was made from. That would create a stir in some quarters. In fact he thought he knew some people who would buy the blueprints merely to destroy them, in order to safeguard their own industry . . . It was just a pity that he had not yet found the prints; he was certain that he would find them in this house; a peasant, such as Stevens appeared to be, would not be likely to use safes or strong-boxes. That room hung about with railway relics was very promising. He wished the visitors would go. The blueprints would fetch a good price, and Lestrange would never guess that he, Sven, was implicated.

It was very amusing, really. He had never seen Lestrange in all the six years of intrigue and violence they had shared. Sven felt no sense of loyalty to the unknown leader of the international gang.

Relaxed still, but watchful, Sven pushed open the cellar door under the stairs, found himself at the top of a flight of

stone steps, flicked his pencil torch on and off and pulled the
door to. Just in time, for he heard voices and then running
footsteps approaching from the living-room.

He watched the crack round the door.

Little sound penetrated the thick panelled door, but he saw
a sliver of light appear and disappear as the hall light went on
and off.

He waited.

The light came on again, then went off. Again Sven waited
patiently. He was an extremely patient person; it was his
stock-in-trade; he did not mind waiting all night if necessary.
Once the plans were in his pocket, he could say goodbye to
Lestrange and his plots, murders and mayhem. Home to
Sweden first, Sven planned, then a long, happy retirement
somewhere warm and safe, with his family.

He smiled.

He heard footsteps on the stairs above his head, then a
series of distant bangs as the doors were shut. He listened
intently for a while, then, thinking all was safe and still, he
pulled at the cellar door.

It resisted.

He directed the torch beam at the door edge, searching for
the knob. He ran a hand down the door.

There was neither knob nor handle.

He was trapped in the cellar.

Sven ran through the possibilities. There were not many. A
window perhaps? No—he remembered now the heavy growth
of an old climbing rose, with prickles like shark's teeth,
covering the barred window. He had been careless, the result
of working for himself. Lestrange left nothing to chance, but
he, Sven, had done.

He must escape. Lestrange had ways of dealing with people
who allowed opportunism to overcome total dedication to The
Cause. The gang must never know that he had burgled the

Stevenses' house. Sven realised now that he could have jeopardised the whole operation, had he found and taken the plans . . .

Desperately, he kicked the door. If only he could open the blasted thing. Somebody must have shot the bolt—interfering busybody . . .

He walked awkwardly down the steps, his rucksack catching the treads of the main staircase above. At least he had had the sense not to leave his belongings behind. He located the faint oblong of the window and pushed vainly against the five iron bars, willing now to risk the shark's teeth.

Defeated and increasingly alarmed, Sven shone his torch round the cellar and so discovered Big Duggy's store of home-made wine.

Gloomily he surveyed the rows of dusty bottles. He wondered how often anybody came down here; how long could he expect to be stuck in this dismal hole? And, more pressing—who would rescue him: Stevens or Lestrange?

He would just have to make the best of things, he supposed; bide his time.

Against his better judgement, Sven reached for a bottle.

Lee and Ginger disobeyed standard practice and tried unsuccessfully to reach Sven on the RT, to check the position of the still-missing boys. It was Sven's boast that he knew if a fly moved on any territory he was surveying.

They were not to know that Sven was surveying a bottle of golden mead at that very moment; that he would take no further part in the action.

One minor but useful link in Lestrange's chain had snapped.

9

'I suppose this old wreck'll work? What about oil?' Simon asked uneasily, in a low voice, as he climbed gingerly on to the narrow seat along one side of the railmotor. 'You're sure it's OK?'

'I bunged oil in this morning before you showed up—I told you! She's not a Rolls-Royce—never was. She wants doing up properly, but she'll not fall apart on us. I—er—I didn't want the Cubbys let loose with a spanner. You know what they're like—at least, what Tim's like.. Anyway, I greased and oiled everything, sort of a bodge-up till we can do it properly—or the Society . . . So she'll start OK—but don't think you can just sit there like Lord Muck—you'll have to move the points before we can get out on to the running line.' Because the railway was Duggy's life—his world—he felt in charge of the situation. He shrugged, acknowledging Simon's misgivings.

'Aye—it'll be all right, man—I mean—what can happen on an empty line? There's not going to be anything coming the other way—or the same way, come to that. And once the line's officially open, we'll never get another chance, although we're not doing this just for fun—not like we thought this morning. That was daft. If we want to get down to Lambley fast, to find the others, this is the only way. I mean, it'd be useless going down on the road. Lambley station is miles from the main road. Bikes would be hopeless, 'specially in the dark. And besides, we're not likely to meet that Range Rover lot on the railway . . . and Cathy's handgrip was on the path beside the railway, don't forget.'

This was an unusually long speech, coming from Duggy. He cast a nervous glance round the railmotor.

'Better push it out then coast down the line a bit—in case there's somebody about—you never know . . . '

Simon opened his mouth to say something on the lines of: 'You've changed your tune.' Then he thought better of it. He remembered the sort of day Duggy had had; he swallowed hard.

Duggy had the key in his palm. 'I'll push—you unlock the clamp on your side—here's the key . . . Now! Move the points!'

The railmotor moved easily on to the main line. Duggy

jumped on to the driver's platform, all fear forgotten in the excitement of being in control of the machine.

He glanced back in Simon's direction. 'Right! Now move the points back and fit the clamp . . . quick, Si! It's getting away on us!'

Simon threw the points lever back, locked them, raced after the railmotor and took a running jump into the shadows. He landed with a thump on the ledge alongside the body of the railmotor. Duggy grabbed his arm in case he overshot, but after an initial loss of balance he held on to the metal bar put there for the purpose, and steadied himself.

It was everything they had imagined it to be. Exhilarated, they rushed through the evening on humming wheels.

Here and there beyond the track they glimpsed glistening burns and startled eyes of cattle and sheep looking to see what beast was charging down amongst them. Once a pony squealed and raced up over the skyline, his mane and tail flying, his bony legs seeming too slight to carry his winter-fat and shaggy body.

Behind, willows and birches soughed in their wake. The spicy scent of flowering currant, of growing things, of spring itself, rose from the lineside. A low full moon cast a bright silver light over the valley, touching the already silver birch-bark, making cobwebs of wire fences and of the track.

'Chas was wrong,' Simon thought, remembering a previous argument over the colour of the lines. 'Cathy's right, it *is* silver after all. The moon's making everything silver—like Midas, only it's silver and not gold.'

Duggy switched the engine on at the beginning of the short uphill section just below the first viaduct; burning oil and exhaust fumes and chugging engine noises drowned out some of the view and all of the night sounds.

Familiar farms and fells took on a new aspect, seen from the railway. The railmotor rattled over the skew bridge at

Burnstones, gradually picking up speed. Mileposts slipped past; underbridges and overbridges loomed ahead then were swallowed up as they sped down the line.

It seemed to Simon as if the railmotor was still, and everything about them moving towards it; at the same time he was aware of the sensation of speed. Suddenly he felt dizzy and found that his hands were locked on to the metal bar so tightly that it was a conscious effort to relax them.

It was impossible to judge their speed: too fast, Simon reckoned. He glanced at Duggy in the moonlight; his expression was a mixture of reckless excitement and terror.

'I say, Duggy—I hope you know how to stop this thing!' Simon yelled, but if Duggy heard, he took no notice.

Then the engine stuttered for a yard or two, picked up, stuttered again, and the motor ran on towards Lambley.

Suddenly the engine cut out.

Duggy groaned into the near-silence: 'Please don't let it stop here!' He need not have worried . . . 'Si! We've no brakes! What am I going to do? Must be a centrifugal clutch—I can't stop! We'll just have to try and run into the loop this side of the station.'

Duggy's mind was totally absorbed, thinking of a way out. There was no room for fear; that came later . . .

Simon's spine prickled as he realised what he had to do. Duggy was saying: 'Sit tight, and when I say jump—jump! Unlock and change the points to the siding, the same as you did at Slaggyford. If we miss the siding and keep going we'll go over the viaduct and mebbe on to the Broomhouse section, then there'll not be much to stop us going down the cutting and on to Haltwhistle. We can't jump for it. We can't leave the railmotor anywhere on the line 'cos it could cause an accident on Monday. Si, we've got to get into that siding.'

Duggy peered along the line, searching desperately for the points into the sidings.

Simon crouched, one hand gripping the metal bar down the corner of the railmotor, every muscle taut, like a cat waiting to pounce outside a mouse-hole. He was going to jump, as far in front as he could.

He tried to remember the drill for falling—what was it again? Roll into a ball, head tucked in, bend knees and relax—*relax*!

But he wasn't going to fall.

'JUMP . . . NOW! Run like blazes!' Duggy shouted.

Simon flung himself on to the lineside, and aware of the railmotor rumbling alongside, he ran as he had never run, to outdistance the motor. He stumbled over a sleeper but regained his balance. He dived at the points and fumbled with key and clamp

But he was too late. He jumped clear as the railmotor shot past. Then suddenly all went quiet.

'Oh, no—a derailment,' Simon groaned.

He ran down the line and saw the railmotor standing on the siding with wheels embedded in a long sand drag made of wooden planks fitted either side of the rails, to form boxes and filled with sand. How had the railmotor got into the siding?

'That was great, Simon,' shouted Duggy. 'What precision timing!'

Simon gasped. 'But I didn't change them,' and walked back to the points, which were locked open to the siding and must have been set that way as a safety measure in case of runaways.

'We should have known how the points would be set, in case some fool tries to do a run down to Haltwhistle before the line's open.' Duggy said with unconscious irony. 'Hope they remember to open them on Monday morning, else the passengers'll all end up making sandcastles.'

Duggy jumped down beside Simon; they exchanged shaky grins.

'Phew! Wouldn't like to do that too often,' Simon said. 'I thought the engine slowed these things if the brakes failed.' He kicked the railmotor, then remembered he was wearing trainers.

'Well, it helps a bit—drags—else you couldn't have got ahead the way you did. Only this one must have a centrifugal clutch, so it doesn't brake. As soon as the engine revs drop, the transmission's free to coast away,' Duggy explained. 'Anyway, I thought you were the mechanic . . . '

'Doesn't look as if we'll be able to use this machine again tonight. We'll just have to shank it back home,' Simon said.

They surveyed the railmotor.

'Could be dirt in the carb, I suppose—or rust. It might settle if we leave it a bit—we can try and start it later.' But Simon was doubtful. 'It's all we can do, anyway—we'll just flatten the battery if we keep trying to start it. Come on—let's see if we can find any sign of Cathy and the Cubbys. We can walk along the ashy path to the station, see if we can find any clues: tyre-marks, or something—anything . . . ' He held the top wire of the railway fence. 'Hop over—I'm not standing here like a stooky all night.'

But they found no trace of Cathy or her bike—or the Cubbys, on the path alongside the line where Melly had found the handlebar grip. The two red-brick houses on the low side were in darkness; but they were only 'weekenders' and it was early in the year for visitors.

'Let's take a look round the station,' Simon suggested, wishing he could get rid of the feeling of doom which had settled on him again, like a wet blanket. 'You never know, they might be in the station-house. You know what Cathy's like—she could have met somebody she knows, visitors—the same ones come back year after year. They might've asked her back or something . . . ' He knew as he spoke that Cathy would never go off without leaving a message of some kind.

'Bit early for visitors, anyway. Old Basil's wife keeps the station house shut all winter.' He brightened momentarily. 'Mebbe with the line opening on Monday, she'll have let it this weekend. Can't think of anything else,' he finished miserably.

Silently, they walked on, their earlier forebodings magnified as they realised how difficult it would be to find the missing trio in the dark.

'I wish we'd phoned your Mum or somebody when we had the chance. There's not a lot they could do now, is there? We'll have to wait till morning to tell the grown-ups—and they're not going to be too pleased. I mean, we have no idea where they really went, apart from the handlebar grip—that's our only clue..' Simon said. Duggy did not know how to reply, so he kept his mouth shut in a straight line.

Moonlight shone fully on the river to their right and beyond, on the fells, where remote farmhouse lights twinkled. On their left the ground rose sharply; the thickly-wooded slope above the station house and buildings was in deep shadow. Ahead of them the moonlight glanced off the grey stones of the great sweeping curve of the Lambley Viaduct which spans the South Tyne on graceful, slender arches.

Like steel to magnet, they went towards the viaduct.

Suddenly Simon crouched down, dragging Duggy with him; he dug an elbow into Duggy's ribs. 'What's that?' he hissed. 'On the viaduct yonder—like a long silvery thread. Now it's gone. Mebbe I just imag—no, there it is again.'

'Aye, I see it now. Could be signal wires, mebbe—no on second thoughts, they haven't connected any of the signaling yet.'

Duggy half-closed his eyes and glared at the viaduct wall, as if willing it to produce something.

'I'll bet we wouldn't have noticed it in daylight. The

moonlight's just catching the inside edge of the wall. It moved though—the wire, I mean—sort of twitched. And there's no wind . . . ' They exchanged meaningful glances. 'It can't be signal wires anyway—they wouldn't have shown above the wall and it can't have twitched by itself. Come on, Si—let's take a closer look!' Unconsciously they spoke in whispers since noticing the wires, although there was no sign of anybody lurking; but sound, they knew, carries easily on still, moonlit nights.

The ashy path came to an end and joined a public path which turned right and meandered through the station house orchard beyond.

They climbed the fence on to the railway and ran along the ballast, scarcely aware of their noisy progress, which made nonsense of their whispered conversation.

So intent were they on investigating that they failed to notice the running, crouching figures keeping pace like shadows, on the station platform high on their left. At the last minute, the shadows accelerated. Simon glanced up—too late. A shifting-spanner caught him on the back of the head and he crumpled. His limp body was carried along to old Basil's garden shed and dropped inside.

Duggy avoided his shadow, being further from the platform; rolled over a low hedge and down into the shadowy orchard, coming to rest behind a row of white-painted bee-hives. The now ruined hedge was a thick bed of bee balm; Duggy knew that he would never forget that sharp, lemony scent. He was grateful to old Basil for planting the balm at the end of the wire fence; he hoped it would recover. He would have been a good target, had he had to climb a fence. He was grateful to Simon for being next to the platform: first in line of fire. Duggy had caught a glimpse of Simon being dealt with. He had never been so frightened for Simon and for himself—Duggy was not easily frightened.

He tried to pretend that he wasn't present; that he was elsewhere; that this wasn't happening; that Simon hadn't been pole-axed.

He waited.

His heartbeat sounded like a drum against the earth under the grass. He made out vague movements along the platform; heard a door bang: Basil's shed door. He realised that it banged on Simon, and wondered why? Why them?

His turn next.

He was on his own.

10

Half of Duggy's mind filed Cathy, Simon and the twins under
'Missing, believed locked in garden shed by thugs unknown'.
The other half wondered how the heck he was going to get
out of this . . .

Then he heard a sliding crunch as somebody jumped off
the platform and came across the line towards the balm
hedge.

'Yis can't get away—and I can see yis—I'll shoot if yis
moves.' It was the voice of Ginger.

Duggy cowered down inside his boiler suit. He guessed that
Ginger couldn't have seen him; if he had, he would have
jumped on him right away instead of hesitating. Quickly
Duggy ran through his options. Move and be shot. He didn't
doubt that Ginger would shoot. His voice had been
cold—emotionless. Well, don't move then, he told himself.

He knew that it was only a matter of time before Ginger
spotted him. Run for it—dive into the Tyne. He remembered
boulders on the river bed—on the steep hill, almost a cliff
edge, leading down to the water. He changed his mind.
Eastwards lay the cliff and the river; northwards the viaduct;
southwards the exposed ashy path; westwards the platform,
the station and Ginger.

There was no way out.

Might just as well give up now.

He had no weapon, apart from a smallish spanner or two. It

was a quiet night; Ginger would hear or see the least movement and shoot at it.

There seemed little else to do except surrender. And all the time he thought why? why? why?

Then, with sudden inspiration, he thought of the thousands and thousands of bees above and about his head, milling about in their hives.

Rapidly he ran through what he knew about bees. It didn't ammount to much, he realised dismally. He didn't even know if they flew at night if disturbed—or if they worked a night shift in the hive, processing the pollen and nectar gathered during the day. He remembered hearing bumblers droning about the garden late of a summer evening; but honey-bees?

His Dad had exchanged bottles of mead for great amber slabs of old Basil's heather honey, last back-end, and that was about all he knew about bees.

Ginger had the look of a man who didn't know much about country matters.

Well, Duggy decided, he had nothing to lose.

Keeping his head well down, he shouted: 'Let me go, else I'll kick these bee-hives over. They'll sting you to death—in minutes!' he added, recalling a horror film about killer bees.

Incongruously, a nightjar chattered in the silence.

Ginger, also recalling the killer-bee film, said hoarsely: 'Bees?'

'Millions,' Duggy confirmed.

'Holy Saints!' Duggy imagined that Ginger crossed himself before asking: 'But shure, will they not sting you first? Yis is closer to them.'

His voice was emotional all right now, Duggy noticed.

'I know about bees. They always go upwards, and you're above them now. And they like bee balm—that's why they call it that, I suppose—that hedge is balm and they'll go for it, and you . . . They'll not half be mad at being disturbed . . . You'll be a gonner in a few seconds. I can hear them buzzing now.'

'You're bluffing.' But Ginger's voice was uncertain. 'I'll be shot anyway, if I let yis get away.'

'But why? What've we ever done to you lot? You've just coshed one of my mates—mebbe more—and we haven't done anything wrong.'

'Yis'll not be harmed if yis come quietly'

'But you just said you'd shoot me if I didn't give myself up. That'd harm me.' What a creep, Duggy thought. It was much later that the incongruity of their conversation struck him.

'Ach well—we only want youse kids out of the way 'til after Monday-' Ginger realised that he had said too much and began to bluster. 'No deals now, c'mon, else I'll shoot.'

Duggy recognised the cold menace in Ginger's voice; he also heard the twang as Ginger climbed over the wire fence, evidently avoiding the balm—and the bees. Quickly Duggy pulled his socks over his boilersuit legs, put his face deep down into the damp grass under one of the hives, and grabbed a leg on the corner of the base of the hive; at the same time he lifted one shoulder, and heaved.

As the hive went over, it separated into four 'lifts', so that the base, containing the brood chamber, remained over Duggy's head. He bent his arms over his head, protecting his ears from the roaring column of bees intent on revenge.

Ginger, caught with one leg either side of the fence, stood no chance.

Even if he could have run away, the bees would have followed; they disliked the smell of fear which hung about him, but most of all they disliked him just for being there.

Ginger opened his mouth to scream as the first sting sank in, then he shut it and scrambled over the fence, up on to the platform and into the station-house, with his nimbus of bees.

Duggy decided that he would most likely be their next target. He rolled over behind the remaining hives and, keeping low, ran towards the cliff top, intending to climb down the rocks and make his way along the river, into which he could plodge should the bees follow him; it would be cold.

He hoped the garden shed was bee-proof; he wouldn't like to be Si if it wasn't . . .

Then he slipped, snatched at some loose stones, lost his balance; and his head connected with a jagged boulder.

Duggy lay all night on a ledge above the river.

Next morning, an early dog-walker wondered at the railmotor parked in the siding. He saw the overturned bee hive; the bees clustered about their queen in the brood chamber. He accelerated, dragging his terrier over the footbridge under the viaduct. This was when he found Duggy. He carried Duggy with surprising ease into his house in the village, having checked that the lad had sustained no obvious structural damage.

Duggy came to on the Good Samaritan's sofa, in front of a good fire. He sat up cautiously. He ran a hand over his aching head and found a bump the shape and consistency of a small hairy tortoise. Immediately a cup of hot, sweet, strong tea was produced by a middle-aged, slightly built woman in a blue tweed suit and hat.

Silently, she watched him gulping the scalding tea. He wondered if she was coming or going, all dressed up as she was. He felt much better, if slightly muzzy, until he remembered about Simon, and Ginger and the bees.

'That's done the trick,' he said, handing over the cup and saucer and heading for the door. 'Thanks very much for—for bringing me here. How? I mean, you couldn't have carried me here?'

She shook her head.

'My husband—and if you're thinking of going, you are doing no such thing! You're not fit to go out yet—you seem to have had a nasty fall.' Mrs. Samaritan pushed him gently back to the sofa. 'Have you far to go? And I would dearly love to know how you came to be on that ledge . . . We'll run you back home, later.'

'Well, thanks, but my friends are in the village—just a few minutes' walk—and I feel fine now, honest,' Duggy assured her, telling himself that this was the truth, in a way. His friends were in the village, or at least one of them was, and he did feel better.

'Well, have some more tea then, and I'll bring you some breakfast—that will set you up! Dear knows how long you lay out there in the cold and damp.' And she hurried off, to reappear with a tray full of dishes of bacon, eggs, toast, fried bread, tomatoes, mushrooms, sausages, marmalade and honey. Almost, Duggy thought, as if she had expected a visitor for breakfast. He found that he was extremely hungry, although he decided to omit the honey.

'You eat up now—we're just off to church, at Haltwhistle. There's no need for you to rush off—we shan't be long.'

Duggy hated being fussed over but, not wishing to be rude, he sat obediently and lifted his knife and fork, then, having heard house and car doors bang, he switched on the small black and white TV, idly watching the screen and wondering if they had driven off yet and hoping they had, so that he could dip the fried bread into his egg-yolk. Suddenly he sat up, spilling coffee on the tray, unnoticed, as he leaned forward attentively to hear the news-reader speak gravely: 'We have received a ransom letter, delivered by hand in the last five minutes, in which the kidnappers of five missing teenagers request the blueprints and the prototype of a revolutionary engine, designed and made by Douglas Stevens, the father of one of the boys, in exchange for the children, who will be returned unharmed on condition that the police are not involved in any way. This assurance will not obtain unless the conditions are met before ten a.m. tomorrow morning, May Day. We have so far been unable to contact the parents of the missing children, but we do ask them, and the public, not to approach anyone acting suspiciously, as this may jeopardise the safety of the children. As soon as more details are available we shall, of course, interrupt our normal programmes to give them.'

By the time the message ended Duggy was on his feet in front of the screen, shielding it from the hall door, in case Mrs. Whoever-she-was came back and started wittering. But the couple had already departed for church.

Funny, that, pushing off and leaving a complete stranger in the house.

Duggy stared at the screen, his tray forgotten. The announcer was saying: 'The police are investigating the theft of a red Range Rover from outside a Hexham garage. The Rover was found abandoned in Alston station yard, having been seen in the area recently. It is believed to have been stolen by three men at present living in the Alston Moor area. Anyone with information about the vehicle or its occupants is asked to contact the police.' A picture was displayed of Alston station yard and the Rover with its trade plates still covered with mud, then the weather forecast came on and Duggy turned the sound down.

His first thought was to telephone his mother. Would this cottage have a phone? It was only a portable TV—might just be weekend folk, although the house felt warm and lived-in. There was a phone in the kitchen. His mother answered in a tearful sort of voice, but she cheered up quickly enough when she heard Duggy's terse message: 'Mum, listen, the people here—I don't even know their name, but they brought me here after I had a fall. Well, they've gone off to Haltwhistle and they're bound to talk to folk at church—they'll mention me, and somebody's bound to have heard the local news, and they might put two and two together . . . Now, the people who have Simon and the others—they likely think they have me as well according to the news—it's a bit complicated but I'm free. I'm OK. It's a long story, but the man who chased me said he would be in trouble if he let me go, only he might be stung to death by now, but I fell and kind of lost sight of him . . . Now, Mum, don't tell anybody I'm safe. Don't tell anybody I've phoned 'cept Dad. I'm safe as long as this gang doesn't know I'm free—they'll try and find me if they know I'm on the loose. It said on the news that five were kidnapped, so that includes me, Simon, Cathy, Tim and Chas . . . They'll get desperate if I turn up safe and sound at home—dear knows what they'll do to the others. I'm going to see if I can find them. It's Dad's new loco, you know. That's what they're after. They'll swop us for it, and the plans, and I s'ppose with me being me, I'll be the one they want most. They'll expect Dad to give them the loco in exchange. There's only today and tonight, so the gang'll think the police'll never find us—they could look for months and never find us. Dad mustn't give up, Mum! He can't give up now. Tomorrow's launching day, so just tell him what I've told you—he'll understand.'

'Well, it's more than I do!' his Mother replied, and, incredulous, reluctant but loyal, she agreed. 'What a weekend this has been—what with the break-in and everything,' she sighed. 'But as long as you're safe—well, I suppose it'll be all right. There's been hordes of policemen going up to Alston—looking for you, likely. Oh, I almost forgot! I found a drunken man in the cellar this morning. The police took him away, but he was unconscious. He'll likely be something to do with your gang—I wish I could understand what's going on.'

'You could phone Mrs. Tate and Mrs. Cubby, if you like, but tell them not to worry and not to tell the police. All that matters is that Unicus is safely launched tomorrow.' Duggy hung up.

11

When Chas realised that somebody had crept up from behind the Land Rover and was boding him no good, he prepared for retaliatory action, but the large bag came as a surprise. The bag, though roomy, clung: stifling, claustrophobic. You can't, he discovered, fight from inside a roomy plastic sack. He felt a rope tightening round his ankles, so that he lost his balance, then round his waist and arms. With great presence of mind, he took in a great gulp of air, filling his lungs so that when he breathed out again there was a slight play on the rope round his middle. The bag had a mesh panel at the front, so there was no danger of suffocation, but that did not detract from the total horror of being tied up and dumped in the back of a Land Rover.

Equally surprised, Tim kicked out and shouted, but was overcome. The bag seemed to sap his energy and he soon realised that it was hopeless to resist. Subsequently, a third bag was added. They heard a crash and guessed it was a bike being thrown into the trailer.

An uncomfortable ride followed, and another pause, but at last the vehicle pulled up and they were dragged out and on to what sounded like a hollow wooden floor. Somebody propped the sacks, sitting up, one to a corner. A door banged.

'You there Chas? What d'ye reckon this is about? What's going on?' Tim's voice was muffled and desperate.

'Hanged if I know. But don't interrupt—I'm planning what

to do to the morons who've done this—I'm only half way through . . . .'

'We'll have to get out of this, Chas. I can't stand being shut up like this—not being able to see or move.'

'Me too,' Cathy joined in unexpectedly.

'It would be bad enough if we'd done something to deserve it. But at least we can talk—and I'm dying for a drink.'

'Quiet!' an unfamiliar voice ordered. 'You can have a drink later—but you gotta keep quiet.'

'I'm not keeping quiet! You'll have to let us go. You can't keep us here. Who d'ye think you are anyway? The police 'n' everybody'll be looking for us. They'll find us, then you'll be for it! And I just hope they hang you, only they don't any more . . . '

'Cathy—shut up,' Chas said sharply. 'You'll only make things worse.'

'She just did,' the voice snapped. 'Settle down—you can't escape. Just be quiet. I want an absence of noise, else I might have to give you something more.'

It turned out to be a long, miserable, drinkless afternoon and evening.

Chas spent his time in gradually working his long thin arms so that he could reach into his anorak pockets. He had no means of knowing where their captor was, or if they were being closely watched, but he reasoned that nobody could remain alert for hours on end. There might be more than one person involved; if so, they were not communicating. His moment would come, Chas reckoned. He wanted to be ready when it did. Meanwhile, he reached two long, pickpocket-type fingers into his left pocket and, using them like chopsticks, gradually worked his Scout's knife into the palm of his hand. Having identified the slot in the blade, he inserted a thumb-nail and tried to exert enough pressure to open it. But it was no use; it was a two-handed job. The blade refused to budge. He reversed the knife and tried again from the other side.

Carefully he slid his thumb between the 'taking-stones-out-of-horses'-hooves' spike and the knife and flicked it open, lengthening its reach by a few useful inches. With the point he could slit the sack and undo knots—if he could find them.

He half-wished that Duggy was with them; he never moved without an assortment of tools in his boiler-suit pockets: a useful chap to be kidnapped with. Then he thought, how ludicrous—to wish for someone else to be kidnapped.

Chas wriggled his back against the wall in an attempt to locate the knot in the rope round his middle.

'Hey—you—cut that out—keep your cotton-picking hands still—or else—'

Chas registered that the voice was vaguely American: the t's slurred, the r's exaggerated. Dispirited, he gave up and sat quietly.

In the beginning, all three worried: about family, about Duggy, and about the reason for their abduction. Gradually they became disorientated and only vaguely aware of being there at all; it seemed almost normal to be tied up in sacks. The only reality was the wall behind them, the blackness all about.

Cathy dreamed then, that she was at home at Burnhaugh in her bedroom, where ancient black bog-oak roof timbers framed a tent-shaped ceiling; the room's pink rose-bud wallpaper so faded that it was almost white, but she wouldn't let her Mum change it—ever; white muslin summer curtains were alternately sucked in and blown out of the open sash of the box window, narrowly missing her collection of china horses which cantered along the wide low sill.

She could lie in bed and look out of the window, to where the great rounded hump of the fell opposite filled the window frame—so that it seemed to be a picture frame.

Sometimes the fell would be white with snow, or sparkling with frost; sometimes green, speckled with white lambs; sometimes golden and purple with bracken and heather.

In winter icy fern patterns decorated the window panes, and then was the time to move down to their bedrooms above the kitchen, where warmth from the Rayburn stove filtered up through the wide, polished floorboards. One attic wall was covered by shelves crammed with every book she had ever read; opposite was the massive old clothes press, so big that it must have been built in the bedroom.

Simon's room, next door, in the widest and highest part of the attic, was known in the family as a disaster area. Raw materials of hobbies past, present and future lay in cartons on the floor so that to do a circuit of the bed you had to hurdle over the boxes. Simon would be asleep now, quilt pulled over his head, until prised out by threats or force.

Funny, Cathy thought, Tim and Chas practically live at our place during the school holidays, yet she had never been in their house, except for a glimpse from the back door into their kitchen—a room of gloom: dull black iron stove; bare stone floor; great jars of dried flowers and leaves; doggy blankets on the chairs; no curtains; dishes and pans piled in the sink. 'A tip,' Mum had snorted after her first and only visit, choosing to forget about Si's room.

'But Mum,' Cathy had tried to explain. 'It's trendy—they're all very clever—they'll not be interested in ordinary things—' This statement had not gone down well.

She stretched, yawning; felt for the corner of her Great-Grandma's pink and white Durham quilt, preparing to push it aside and leap out of bed to see what kind of day it was going to be.

But her eyes opened on darkness.

Her hand grasped, not the soft cotton of Great-Grandma Catherine's quilt, but rough plastic. Cathy shut her eyes, tried desperately to escape back into her dream. But she knew that you never could.

Simon joined them later. They heard the door open, the shuffling sound of something being dragged along the floor, then Chuck's voice asking: 'Where's the other one—the Stevens boy? This isn't the one!'

And the reply: 'Ginger was detailed to look after him. He was to be kept separate from the others—he'll be in the station house, next door. Ginger's taking first watch while you sleep—he can see both places from the station house kitchen window. Swap over at eight—that way you'll be OK for tomorrow—Boss's orders.'

'Well, I'm off now—down to Haltwhistle. S'long—see you tomorrow. Nine for ten!' They both laughed.

Vaguely, Chas puzzled over that. 'Nine for ten' sounded like a posh dinner invitation. The door slammed and the four teenagers sank back into lethargy.

Nobody in the shed heard Ginger blunder into the station house, where he lit a cigarette with shaking hands, to try to encourage the bees to go away, then fortified himself with something out of a bottle before setting off, staggering, to the council tip, where his Land Rover was concealed. He sat there for a few minutes, wondering whether to clear off—finish with Lestrange altogether. After all, he had mucked everything up, letting young Stevens get away. He groped for the interior light switch, to see how bad his face was. He couldn't see!

Suddenly he felt faint.

Half paralysed with shock and fear, he put his arms on the steering wheel and rested his grossly swollen head on them. Half-formed notions flitted across his mind. The boy would be too scared to stay near the station buildings. He would hide, or scarper off to the police, although the law could do nothing without dropping the other four kids right in it. No, the law wouldn't risk Lestrange harming the four kids over in the shed. Ginger's danger lay in the gang finding out that young Stevens was still scot-free. If any of the gang saw him in this state they would know that Ginger had failed, for the first time, to carry out his part of the plan. Lestrange's revenge would not be pleasant. Ginger shivered, partly from fear, partly from a kind of fever, as he thought of the extent of

Lestrange's influence. In the end it was money which decided; he would carry on as normal.

He would carry on as if everything had gone to plan. Ginger almost persuaded himself that Duggy was securely tied up in the station house at Lambley.

After all, he reasoned hazily, there was only tonight and tomorrow to get through. At ten on Monday the operation would be over. He could easily bluff it out till then. Even if young Stevens went to the police, they surely wouldn't rubbish the other four kids.

The rest of the gang, except Chuck and himself, had cleared off to near Haltwhistle; they wouldn't know what was going on up at Lambley. They had done what they had to do; conned the police away from Haltwhistle and up to Alston. The cops would be having a fine old time on Alston Moor, searching for the kids.

Then, inevitably, he had a vision of the money Lestrange would be paid for the operation, part of which would be paid into his, Ginger's, Swiss bank account. Damn bees! He took another, longer drink from the bottle.

12

Tim was the action man of the group. Chas was the brain, Tim the brawn, of the Cubby twins. Deprived of action, Tim was forced to think.

Hunger pains had wakened all four; it seemed a long time since the soup and sandwiches.

At first Chuck watched them carefully; they were his insurance. Apart from Ginger, he was on his own. The rest of Lestrange's gang were now gathering together the threads, ready for the big day. The result of meticulous planning would be manifest! 'Hallelujah!' he shouted—inwardly. Funny, he thought, how much cash certain organisations were prepared to pay the likes of Lestrange for this type of operation.

Just a question of knowing the right people and having the right men to do the job. All credit for the planning went to Lestrange, whoever he was. He was the fly in the ointment—or the spider at the centre of the web. You never knew where he was, or even who he was. They said that nobody did, not even his own mother. He was good at disguises.Even smarter, he slipped into the personality of the character he was impersonating. Clever, that.

Occasionally Chuck felt uneasy about the company he kept. He had come a long way from the Arkansas shack where his Mom and Paw still lived—if you called it living. The rocking chair on the back porch; the cotton and rice fields—miles and miles of cotton, all picked by machine now, so there was no work for folk. His palms tingled painfully, just thinking about the hard cotton; the way it looked so soft and fluffy, all burst open, and the way it took the skin off your hands . . . Lordy—if Mom knew how he earned those dollars he sent so regularly—hitting kids over the head with spanners. But he was in too deep now; Lestrange kept his gang together not by loyalty to any cause, but by having a hold over them. They were all criminals—terrorists on Interpol's Wanted list; had been long before Lestrange picked them up.

Chuck yawned; this operation had been easy so far—like taking candy off of kids. Nobody associated terrorists with this part of England—Britain.

Things would warm up Monday, though.

These kids seemed quiet enough. Just as well. Pointless, using violence on kids, although Ginger didn't agree. Lestrange's sacks had turned out OK, too wide and roomy to split—or to be split. He checked that the door was locked and the key on its nail.

He switched off the lamp. The sleeping-pills should have an effect soon. They had pills to make them sleep; pills to wake them up. Ginger would be on watch now. He, Chuck, had to show in Haltwhistle early Monday. By then the kids would be totally disorientated; it would be safe to leave them unguarded. They had no water, though; that worried him. But they couldn't drink through the sacks, and he didn't want to think about what Lestrange would do to him if the kids escaped.

Smart, the way the boss kept his head down and his finger on the pulse—like as if everybody was bugged. The cops would be pulling out all the stops to find the kids—all the mineshafts, coal-drifts and derelict houses on Alston Moor would keep them busy. He grinned.

Then, sleepily, he went over his instructions again. It was always like this; the build-up of tension as the end of the assignment approached. Monday evening, the whole shebang would be on the fishing boat, *en route* from Port Ryan to a small village on the south-eastern coast of Ireland.

After that, none of them knew. Africa, maybe. Be warmer than this God-forsaken hole.

He slept.

Chas stretched cautiously, wriggling his toes and fingers, remembering what had gone before. But no warning voice snarled at him this time.

He bent his knees, felt the sack tighten round his ankles. Still no response.

His cramped hand still gripped the knife; after all, there was nowhere for it to go. Gradually he moved his wrists until his fingertips met. Holding the knife in his palm, he prised open the blade.

This was more than he had been able to do before. Then he realised that the sack ballooned out from his body, except where the rope drew it in, round waist and ankles. His best chance of puncturing it would be round the middle, where the rope would be within reach.

What if the blade jackknifed? Better try the spike first. Holding his breath, he stuck the point into the thick plastic-coated sack.

There was a distinct 'ping'.

He waited.

But Chuck was silent.

Reversing the knife in his hand, he hacked at the now exposed rope as best he could, trying to do it quietly, enlarging the hole in the bag and sawing away until it was large enough to claw his hand through. The rope felt smooth, like sash-cord, but he persevered.

At last, one strand parted. He hacked and pulled until it loosened and his arms were free.

Chas then cut a slit for his eyes.

The shed was in darkness.

No wonder Chuck had heard nothing of his scrabbling about with the knife; he must have gone.

Quickly Chas stooped, groping for the rope round his ankles. In seconds he was free; shaky, but free.

He leaned against the wall, weak with relief. He did a few exercises to bring back circulation to his cramped limbs, then he crouched down on his hands and knees and began to explore, feeling his way along against the batten wall. The floorboards lay at right angles, therefore this must be one of the long walls. Pity: doors were usually in the short end-walls.

Then he noticed a familiar smell: beeswax and honey and apples.

He paused, considering. As far as he knew there was only one beekeeper in the area: old Basil. He had a shed. Chas felt a great bubble of relief in his stomach. It all fitted; they hadn't gone far after being kidnapped. Lambley was within the radius of ten miles or so which he reckoned the Land Rover had travelled. They had, he remembered, turned right at the T-junction, stopped, reversed, then turned left; yes, it definitely fitted. He had tried to time the journey, counting seconds, but had lost count. Still, he was pretty sure he was right. A good place to hide four kidnapped folk—at least until the railway opened. But why? Why should anybody want to kidnap four country kids—or five?

The beeswax scent was stronger now; old Bas kept spare comb and frames, as well as the honey extractor, at the far end of the shed furthest away from the door. No wonder it was dark—the window was shuttered in case the bees got in and started robbing the combs.

Chas sensed something ahead and held a hand out tentatively, kneading the air. He felt a bulging sack—bulging with Tim, judging from the size.

'Tim!' Chas whispered urgently. 'Tim?'

Tim always wakened irritated, hoping the day would go away. Chas felt his twin's head move away as he felt down the sack, searching for the sash-cord.

'Keep still, you idiot,' Chas murmured. 'Else I might do you a mischief.' He found the sash-cord and sawed through it. 'There—stay there till you feel OK to move. Get your circulation going.'

Chas discovered Simon next, lying beside the door.

He was the only one without a sack.

'I think the one called Chuck's near the door, so watch out.' Simon whispered. 'I heard him talking to somebody when I wakened the first time. Something about Ginger being on watch and Chuck sleeping till eight, and then he said: "See you in the morning." No, that wasn't quite it—"Nine for ten", he said, and they laughed. Something like that, anyway—but I got whacked on the head—' His head still ached.

But he got no sympathy from Chas.

'Get that door open—if Chuck comes to we want to be able to see.'

Simon was familiar with Bas's shed, having visited it with Duggy. He knew that the lock was intended to keep people out, not in; it was a huge, old-fashioned affair, with an enormous key, which was superfluous. Simon crooked a finger behind the slot in the door-frame and slid the bolt free of the keep. He opened the door and took a deep breath.

Tim found his own sack and approached the sleeping Chuck. His stubbly blond head was sunk on his chest; nobody could have slept normally through the last few minutes, Chas thought; must be drugged. This sort of thug probably carried a gun. Chas and Tim between them went through Chuck's pockets and found a gun; Tim pocketed it. With deep satisfaction, Tim bagged and bound Chuck, then helped Chas to undo Cathy.

On the way out Tim noticed the key hanging on the nail. He locked the door behind them and, with a mental apology to old Bas, he flung the key as far as he could, into the early Sunday morning gloom.

Shaky and white-faced, avoiding each other's eyes, they leaned against the shed wall, breathing in the cold dawn air, going over what had happened yesterday.

'Well, we can't hang about here. The gang might be about—we don't want to be had again. Come on, into the house.'

'Hang on, Tim. I heard the gang mention Ginger—I think they said he was in the station house—with Duggy! Better have a recce first,' Simon suggested.

'I'm just about past caring who's in what—so long as I can have a drink,' Cathy croaked. She went and peered in the downstairs windows.

Nobody contradicted her: a sign of their demoralisation. Normally they would have stopped Cathy from leaving the shelter of the shed.

Simon did not feel like moving, ever. His head still ached. He watched Cathy, noticed how dirty her face was, even in the half-light. He would have laughed, if his head would stop twirling.

The fresh air had restored Tim and Chas.

'Now for a bit of housebreaking. Old Mrs. Bas'll not mind if we make free, will she? It's an emergency. And it's not as if it's a proper house—it's only for visitors.' Tim fished in his pockets and with a quick grin at Cathy, added: 'You're far too young for this sort of thing—don't look!'

'Never mind her—get on with it!' Chas snapped, glancing about as if expecting the gang to appear out of the dawn.

Tim's eyebrows rose at his twin's unaccustomed edginess, but he said nothing and concentrated on the locked station-house door. He worked at the door for a while with the various items he fished out of his pockets, then at last the lock clicked and the door was open. They went in and snibbed the door.

Again taking the initiative, Chas motioned his twin towards the stairs then padded off to check the downstairs rooms.

They searched the house for Ginger and Duggy but there was no sign of anybody having slept in the rooms.

Reassured, they then consumed water until Chas warned them not to.

'Duggy could've got away; we were just walking along when somebody walloped me on the head. Can't remember anything else.' Simon sat down suddenly and put his head on his arms on the kitchen table.

'I'll see if there's anything in the bathroom,' Cathy said, running upstairs two at a time. She reappeared waving a bottle. 'Aspirin! There's a first-aid box up there. But there's no sign of life—no sheets on the beds. If the gang's been living here they've slept on the floor. Si, I've put some blankets on a mattress. Go on, have a proper nap—you're not much use to anybody the way you are.'

'Good idea!' Chas said, with an approving glance at Cathy. 'And while he's sleeping it off, we'll have a think about Duggy.'

So Simon tottered upstairs and the others sat round the table, glum and subdued once the initial excitement of escaping had receded.

'A cuppa is what we need,' Tim announced. 'And some food—I'm absolutely starving.'

'You'll be lucky,' Chas said. 'You don't expect to find food in here?'

'Well, here's some tea-bags and dried milk. And there's a bag with a bit of flour—urgh, it's all weevilly—but that's all there is.' Cathy opened and shut cupboard doors. 'Salt and pepper, and that's all—definitely. Sort of iron rations, I suppose.'

Chas flicked a light on and off, and filled a kettle when he saw the power was on. 'Well, tea'll be better than nothing,' he grumbled.

'Stop complaining,' Cathy told him. 'Make yourself useful and find some cups'. Cathy made the tea in a metal pot, after first scraping off and washing out a thick green sort of inner jacket; last summer's visitors' last pot of tea.

Tim watched with a wry expression, but he dared not speak.

Chas searched for a clean spoon. 'Typical holiday place!' he muttered, rummaging through a drawer full of cutlery. 'Everything and nothing.'

He stirred dried milk into three cups, swirling it round absently, not quite letting the tea lap over the rim.

'Nectar,' Tim said, emptying his cup at a gulp. 'Or is it ambrosia? I'm so hungry I could eat anything—except weevils.'

Cathy giggled: 'I could make some Billy cake with that flour if only I could catch it.'

'Ah yes,' Chas remembered. 'Those flat things like hub-caps that you have with Indian food.'

'Thank goodness for weevils.' Tim murmured.

Cathy put down her empty cup. 'Listen, I've just remembered, I noticed an old radio in the front room—let's see if we can get Radio Two. There might be some news. I know it's the middle of the night almost, but you never know. Our folks might've noticed that we're missing. I mean, they'll all think we are staying at each other's houses, like we usually do, but if they check up—you know what I mean?'

'Everything's at sixes and sevens this weekend—the Tates are doing their shop, ready for Monday. Duggy's folks are busy with the railway, and preparing to feed all those extra visitors. Our parents were half-going to a farm sale in Yorkshire, staying the weekend, depending on the weather and coming back on Sunday night—that's tonight, isn't it?' Chas asked. 'What a glorious mix-up! But anyway, we're not exactly the stuff that news is made of. And that's the funny thing—I mean Duggy I can understand—with Unicus and all that. I can understand him being kidnapped in exchange for the new loco—but us?'

'Well, Duggy's not here—Si thinks he might have escaped. But we don't know for sure, do we? So where is he? And where's that awful Ginger?' Cathy finished quietly. She felt quite light-headed; by turns giggly and so churned up inside that she couldn't bear to think about what they had been through; what they might still have to go through . . . 'It's funny, isn't it—how we can sit here, drinking tea and joking, while those awful men are somewhere out there—' She waved a slightly shaky hand and smiled a slightly wobbly smile. 'Kidnapping people and putting folk in sacks . . . '

'It's our Dunkirk spirit,' Tim said solemnly. 'When the little ships went over to Dunkirk, the sailors invited what was left of the Army on board by asking: "Any more for the *Skylark*?" But

I bet they were all quaking inside, just like us.'

'All the same, I'd like to know where Duggy is—and if Ginger's with him—or where?'

'Does it matter? I mean, as long as Ginger's not here, where we know he should be, it's a fairly safe bet that he hasn't got Duggy—safeish, anyway. And if any of the gang comes back, I've got this!' With a dramatic gesture, Tim pointed Chuck's gun at the ceiling.

'That's illegal. And dangerous.' Chas jumped up from the table. 'Nobody's allowed a gun without a licence—you should throw that in the Tyne.'

'Listen, Chas.' Tim squared his shoulders and replaced the gun in his pocket. He combed his hair with his fingers: it flopped back over his brow. 'Listen, if it's a choice between the gang and us, it's going to be us! Besides, you were there when I dug the gun out of Chuck's pocket! What did you think I was going to do with it?'

The twins glared at each other.

Not for the first time, Cathy was struck by the un-twinness of the Cubbys. Chas: tall, awkward and skinny, long wavy dark hair hiding most of his pale face and gentle brown eyes—usually gentle, she amended; they weren't always sparkling as they were now; bony wrists, as always, four inches longer than his cuffs; bony purple-socked ankles showing four inches between jeans and shoe-tops.

And Tim: equally tall, but broad and all of a piece; fair, thick, straight hair which he was forever combing back with an impatient hand; dark-lashed, sharp blue eyes; dark, slanting eyebrows; fresh healthy complexion.

Cathy flushed as Tim caught her watching him. She got up to wash the cups.

Tim turned back to Chas. 'Well, us being here is illegal—we broke in, didn't we? Anyway, I'm not going about shooting people. But I'm not letting that gang mess us about either.'

'It's the same as stealing, isn't it? Us being here, I mean, making free with somebody's tea and stuff. How much shall we offer old Bas—?' Cathy began, but Tim interrupted: 'The worst thing anybody can pinch is your freedom. Well, we just had ours pinched.'

'I, for one, wasn't very struck on it.'

'Si was,' Chas murmured. 'Struck—'

'There—you see?' Tim exclaimed. 'The Dunkirk spirit again—laughing at poor old Si's expense.' He leaned back and put his hands in his pockets. 'I hope he's going to be OK.'

They sat in glum silence for a few seconds, then Cathy gave one of her spectacular leaps out of her chair.

'The radio! I might just catch the headlines—it's about six.'

She ran into the small room across the hall and switched on the old wooden-cased radio. After much twiddling of knobs, a Cumbrian voice surfaced from the mishmash of interference.

'. . . headlines again,' the voice was saying. 'There is still no news of the five missing local teenagers and no one is available for comment. All available personnel have joined the search, which is concentrated in the Alston area. It is believed that the deadline for handing over the plans and the revolutionary new loco is still ten o'clock tomorrow morning, May Day. Should we have any further information we shall, of course, interrupt our normal programme. Traffic was held up at Shap early this—' Slowly Cathy reached out and switched off, then she ran back to the kitchen. Suddenly excitement welled up inside her.

'Did you hear? We're kidnapped because of Big Duggy's new loco,' she gasped, pink with emotion. 'It was on the news! Nobody's found Duggy yet, 'cos the radio said five teenagers are missing!'

'Well, it's just what we guessed,' Tim spoke slowly, then he glanced quickly at Chas. 'But we've got to let them think we're still kidnapped. I just hope Duggy realises that as well, wherever he is. We've got to find out what's going on, It'll all just fizzle out if we all show up; the gang'll get away scot- free. They'll mebbe try the same thing on somebody else.'

'We've got to find Duggy,' Chas said flatly. 'Si might remember a bit more of what happened when he wakes up. Meantime I think we should take a look outside—there might be footprints, or signs of a scuffle, on the ballast. Come on, Tim, it's now or never. If we wait till later there'll be all sorts of railway folk about—and mebbe police as well. They'll walk over any marks there might be.'

'But what about me?' Cathy almost panicked. 'You can't just leave me here—'

'Well, somebody's got to stay and keep an eye on Simon—he's your brother, isn't he? And you can watch along the railway from this window. If anybody suspicious shows up—well, you know what to do. Remember the whistle?'

Half-smiling, Cathy nodded and brightened up, remembering their special signal which Chas had perfected when they were much younger and liable to lose their way on the fells, before they had grasped the principles of orienteering. Sometimes their sheepdogs came running at the shrill sound, having mistaken it for the shepherd's whistle.

She cupped her hands round her mouth and drew in a deep breath.

'Not now, you idiot!' Tim said. 'You'll have everybody awake for miles around! It's for emergency only—but for Pete's sake don't panic and do something daft, unless somebody comes near old Bas's shed, or the house . . . Compris? Anybody you don't like the look of—whistle! We'll just be down from the platform yonder—going towards the viaduct . . . Then I think we should wake Si when we come back, then scarper, if there's no sign of Duggy.'

'Scarper, where to?' Chas asked. 'We don't know where Ginger is—he could be nearby.'

'If he's supposed to be here, guarding Duggy, he's probably not far away, waiting to relieve Chuck, according to what Si heard.'

'Well, we know that Chuck is nicely tied up in the shed. What we should do is put ourselves in Ginger's place, and work out what he would do when he failed to get hold of Duggy—which must be what happened, else Duggy would be here.' Tim drew in a sharp breath. 'Here—you don't suppose Ginger's got confused with Lambley and Slaggyford station houses? The gang must know a lot about us. They'll probably know that Duggy's folk are busy elsewhere. They'll know that nobody'd think of Duggy being kidnapped—in his own house! That would explain why Duggy and Ginger aren't here—I mean, Ginger's got to show up to take over guard duty from Chuck—or is it the other way round?—this morning at eight, so, even without Duggy, Ginger's still going to turn up here, otherwise the gang'll know that he's failed. I wish we knew . . . They seem pretty ruthless to me, what with guns and threats and things. I wouldn't fancy being in Ginger's shoes if he ever has to explain that he's lost us! And Duggy—their trump card!'

'And I wouldn't like to be in our shoes if they catch us again.' Cathy stood up, then sat down abruptly, remembering Simon, upstairs. 'Go on then, push off—I don't mind—really. But be quick!' She gave a shaky smile as the twins left. Suddenly the house developed creaks and groans she had not noticed before.

Cathy sat at the window, scarcely breathing, watching the line. Tim and Chas slid out of the back door, flattening themselves against the rough stone wall, feeling vulnerable and ridiculous. Trees on the banking behind the paling fence darkened both house and platform, as they did even in high summer.

They edged along the palings, intending to jump down on

to the ballast and search for any signs of a struggle. Straight ahead was the viaduct. No use going that way, Chas signalled, with a thumbs down: too exposed. The danger would outweigh the advantage of being able to see everything for miles. To the left, a narrow path behind a stone dyke led into the village; few locals used it, except for occasional walkers, and it was so well hidden that most strangers would never see it. The station house garden and orchard lay to the right.

Tim and Chas glanced about, then ran across the platform and down on to the ballast.

The ballast was disturbed. Tim pointed to the far side, where depressions showed where somebody had jumped across the metals. Small twigs were scattered about. Tim picked up one of them and sniffed: bee balm. Bas's bee balm hedge; it had no flowers yet, but the small pale minty leaves had a strong scent. He jumped the low new growth and immediately saw the overturned beehive.

'Chas!' he hissed, waving at the devastation; at the early bees buzzing about their hive.

One glance was sufficient; they ducked and ran, as Duggy had done, towards the river.

And that was how they came to see the dog-walker carrying Duggy in a fireman's lift, up the path into the village.

They dodged behind the wall, relieved that Duggy evidently was free of Ginger but worried in case he was badly hurt. Anxiously they trailed along after Duggy and his rescuer, keeping out of sight, wondering if this was a rescue or another kidnap. Could this man be yet another member of the gang?

They watched through gaps in the stone dyke opposite the cottage as Duggy was carried inside.

Turning to Tim, Chas whispered: 'Nip and tell Cathy we've found him. I'll keep an eye here for say half an hour, then we'll swap.'

Tim nodded and ran off. Arriving at the station house, he succeeded in frightening Cathy into screaming by suddenly appearing outside her window and gesticulating towards the door. She opened the door and waded into him: 'Well, of all the stupid, witless . . . '

'Shut up and listen,' Tim interrupted tersely. 'We know where Duggy is. He's hurt—seems unconscious—but somebody in the village has taken him into a house. Chas is watching it for half an hour, then I'll swap places with him. We don't know what that man'll do—send for a doctor, mebbe, or the law.... Anyway, we'll have to stop him giving the game away. Move over and let me in—or are you going to climb on the roof and tell everybody we're here?' Then seeing how tired and scared she was, he joked: 'Got a crust for a pore hungry tramp, missus?'

'If I had, you wouldn't get it. I'm starving as well', Cathy said, instantly cheerful. 'And I've just realised why we look so awful—we haven't had a wash for ages, and we've been grovelling about in all sorts of muck. I'm off upstairs to have a scrub—you can peer through the net curtains for a change.' And she skipped upstairs before Tim could object.

Tim and Chas took turns at hovering behind the dyke, watching the cottage in what they soon discovered was a strangely deserted village.

They did not know that the village was strangely deserted because, except for a few old or infirm folk, its inhabitants were up at Alston, helping to search the fells, mine-shafts and derelict houses in a desperate attempt to locate the missing teenagers.

Only the Kings, Duggy's Good Samaritans, evidently knew nothing of the exodus. Having recently moved into the village, they had not yet mingled. A thick thuja hedge surrounding the garden obscured all vision; nobody could see in or out. It was obvious that Duggy needed rest and warmth; Mr. King's experience as a member of a Mountain Rescue team qualified him to give first aid. He and his wife were happy to keep an eye on Duggy until he came to.

'He'll have been larking about by the river—stumbled over the rocks—lucky he got off so lightly,' Mr. King observed, tamping his pipe on the hearth.

'There's a job for you, now that we're retired,' Mrs. King said, eyeing the pipe-tamping coldly. 'Form a youth group, teach them climbing, that sort of thing.' She swept the hearth briskly.

'Mm,' said Mr. King. 'I might do just that.'

Simon came to, washed, pulled himself together and padded downstairs, feeling much better. Tim explained to him about finding Duggy and not finding Ginger. Simon listened intently, then glanced at his watch. 'I'll take a turn at watching for Duggy, but I reckon we shouldn't be here.... Tell you what. It's pushing eight o'clock—I'll have a look round from the top of the hill, through the trees. Nobody'll see me—not with all that undergrowth. You can see for miles from up there—along both the main road and the railway. I might just see something interesting, like Ginger. He was supposed to be changing over with Chuck at eight, wasn't he? Right! So if he's about, he'll show up. If not, he's pushed off. See you!' He swallowed the fresh tea Cathy had made, pulled a face and put the cup down. 'Yuk!' He slipped out of the door, over the fence and disappeared into the dark wood.

Tim stared morosely at his own cup.

'What did you put in this?' he asked, swirling the pale green liquid about.

'Never mind, just drink it—it's good for you. Refreshing and reviving—Auntie Ada used to make it and she was ninety-six when she died!' Cathy had remembered about balm tea and had dashed out to pick some leaves from old Bas's hedge.

'She might have been here yet if she hadn't drunk this stuff.' Tim ducked away and ran to relieve Chas. He met his twin running towards him along the narrow path.

'What's up?' Tim whispered.

'They've gone—towards Haltwhistle—black car,' Chas panted. 'Duggy wasn't with them....'

They stared at each other, fear flickering at the back of their eyes.

'Funny time to take off,' Tim said. 'And a complete stranger in their house....'

As one man, they turned and sprinted up the garden path and pressed the door-sneck. As expected, the door was locked.

'Well, it would be. If Duggy's out for the count, they would hardly leave the door open. What about the back door?' Tim shook his head.

'Only one door—try a window.'

The windows were locked and double-glazed; totally break-in-proof.

'Looks as if they're nervous—it's like Fort Knox! Now what do we do?'

Chas shrugged.

'An open pantry window, mebbe?'

While Chas scouted round the back, Tim peered through the windows, shielding his eyes with a cupped hand. He saw Duggy hunched in an armchair with a plate of bacon and eggs on his knee, watching television. Tim banged on the window and waved his arms, but Duggy took no notice.

Meanwhile Chas had found a small pantry window open and insinuated his thin body into it. There were a few casualties, mainly cups, but at least he was in the house. He unscrewed the heavy iron lock on the door and opened it for Tim, and they both went into the living-room.

Pale but grinning, Duggy stared at them.

'Well, I'm blowed,' he gasped. 'I've been trying to get out and couldn't. Never thought of taking the lock off....'

Tim switched the TV off.

'And here's us worried in case those folk had done you in or something—and here's you stuffing yourself as usual. It can't be good for you....' He made a bacon, egg and toast sandwich, and mumbled through it: 'You've no business looking so ordinary—if you could've seen yourself a few hours ago.'

'Where've they gone in such a hurry anyway, the people who rescued you?' Chas asked, helping himself to a piece of fried bread and a couple of sausages.

Tim fetched two extra cups and poured coffee.

'Church', Duggy explained. 'Haltwhistle. They're canny folk —kind and all that, at least she is. I didn't see much of him but he must have carried me back here. She didn't half make a fuss....'

'We'll be off as well, just as soon as we've cleared this lot—better take a bite for the others, eh?' Tim started on toast and marmalade. 'They'll be mad if we don't.'

'If these folk are as kind as all that, they'll want us to make a sandwich or two—we can pay them back later.' Chas went to hunt in the kitchen and returned with plastic bags full of fruit cake and thick sandwiches with plum jam oozing out.

'They'll just think you have a boisterous appetite,' he grinned at Duggy. 'Come on, you two—'

Suddenly they froze as the door was pushed open. It was Simon. He hesitated in the hallway.

'Thank goodness—it's only you.' Tim recovered first. 'Come in, man.' Then he saw Cathy's face looking over Simon's shoulder and his voice sharpened.

'What's up? Has Ginger turned up? Why have you left the station house?'

'Found Ginger!' Simon's laconic statement had a profound effect on Tim.

'Found? Where?' he snapped.

The strain began to tell—Chas sat on the arm of a sofa, leaning forward so that his spaniel-ear hair hid his face; he clasped his hands tightly between his knees.

Tim glowered at Simon. Cathy was ready to burst into tears.

It was left to Duggy to ask quietly: 'Come on, lad. What's the matter? We're all a bit edgy—but where is Ginger?'

Simon swallowed hard.

'He's in a Land Rover, beside the tip. He's swollen up like a paddock!' He curved his hands round his head. 'His head's all sort of puffed out and his fingers are like sausages—horrible, he is.'

'The bees!' Duggy shouted. 'They must have stung him—and he'll be allergic. Some people are. Folk can die, if the sting's in the right place....'

'I suppose you mean in the wrong place.' Tim sounded pleased. 'Well, at least Ginger's out of the running, and we've got Chuck.'

'How did you find Ginger, Si? I mean, is he—?' Chas hesitated.

'Is he dead?' Cathy asked in a scared voice. Simon had appeared at the station house window and dragged her up to the village without telling her anything—as usual, she thought.

'Well, I noticed the Land Rover when I climbed up the hill behind the station—and it seemed a funny time and place for a farmer to be about. Then I remembered that the gang had a Land Rover, so I left the wood and crawled over the top of the tip so's I could look down, and that's how I saw Ginger's head, leaning on his arms, on the steering-wheel. It was pretty hideous....'

'He is anyway,' Cathy murmured. 'Hideous—but I'm not half glad you found him Si. I've been expecting him to pop up, waving a gun.'

'Two can play at that game,' Tim said with a sly glance at Chas.

'Yes, but he'll have had more practice than you have,' Chas retorted

'Quick, pour yourself some coffee, Cath, while we catch up on what we've all found out,' Simon said, sensibly. 'We'll have time before these folk come back. It'll take them a bit to get to Haltwhistle and back—then there's the service.... You know, they're bound to tell somebody at Haltwhistle about finding Duggy.'

'Then it'll only be a question of time before somebody connects Duggy with the "missing teenagers", and reports him to the police. Hurry up with that coffee, Cath, get it down you.'

Cathy put her tongue out but gulped her coffee, then asked casually, 'Why have they gone to church at Haltwhistle when there's a perfectly good church here?'

'Well, they can go wherever they like, I suppose.'

'Come on,' Simon said impatiently, making for the door.

'It's all right saying come on—but where to? Where is there to go?' Cathy objected. 'I know we can't stay here, at Lambley, but we can't be seen walking about either. There might be police all over Slaggyford by now—they'll be getting desperate now. They don't give in to blackmail, you know—not even for us!'

'She's right,' Simon agreed. 'Besides, we've got to keep an eye on Ginger—he's not going to stay in the Land Rover is he, once he comes to?'

'*If* he comes to—or *when* he comes to. We don't know how bad he is. But he's got a problem too,' Chas said, swinging his hands loosely between his knees. 'He can't seek help from the rest of the gang without them finding out that he's failed to get Duggy. We've got to stop him getting in touch with any of them. He might try to get back into Bas's shed to see if

Chuck'll get him off the hook—and then, come to think of it, Chuck's in the same boat now, since we've all escaped.'

'We've got to wait till it gets dark before we can do anything. We've got to plan.' Cathy said. 'But where can we go?'

'There's only one thing to do!' Tim announced, looking from one to the other, enjoying watching their expressions change as he went on: 'We've got to chuck Ginger in with Chuck—if you see what I mean— and the sooner the better. That way we know where they both are.'

Simon, as usual, resented being pushed into one of Tim's schemes, but even he could see that they had to put Ginger safely out of the way.

'OK,' he agreed reluctantly. 'I'm game.'

'Aye, but how are we going to cart a great lump like him from the tip along to the shed? We'll need a crane,' Duggy said. 'We'll never prise him out of the Land Rover—he'll be a pretty tight fit, I'd say.'

'Well, you're a pretty useless lot, I must say,' Tim exclaimed. 'All we need do is drive the Land Rover—complete with Ginger—along from the tip and yank him out on to the platform. Surely we can manage that? Cathy can open the shed door, we carry him in, bung him in a sack, lock the door, then drive the Land Rover somewhere where it won't be found.'

'Melly's garage!' Cathy yelled, excited at having found a solution. 'Nobody'd ever think of looking for it in a garage.'

There was a short silence while the boys remembered who Melly was.

'Melly? Oh, *that* Melly. Different league from us—her Dad won't want a grotty old Land Rover parked next to his car.'

'Aye, he drives one of those posh foreign jobs—a Porsche, isn't it? Not that I know much about him.... Sounds as if you do, Chas.'

'No—but you know, Duggy, folks talk....'

'Yes, and what they say is: Why did a rich young couple adopt a Jamaican girl, when they're never at home to look after her? As Mum says: an Irish wolfhound's no substitute for parents.' Duggy's Mum gleaned a lot of gossip from the Alston shop. 'You see—' Duggy looked embarrassed but he continued: 'Mum always wanted a daughter—as well as me, I mean.'

There was a short silence in which the others tried to imagine a female Duggy.

'Well, Melly's nice. And so's her dog—you can say what you like about her parents, but Melly doesn't seem to mind being on her own. Her parents are often there and she has loads of expensive things—so there.'

'Calm down, Cath! We're not saying she isn't nice, 'cos she is,' Simon broke in impatiently. 'Anyway, it was our Mum who said Melly was just another pretty possession! Her parents have just about everything money can buy . . . Well, are we going to do something, or not?'

'Melly's folk are away abroad again—that's why I've been going down on my bike, to keep her company . . . She'll be chuffed if we ask her to help us.'

'A garage would be handy—Keeper's Lodge is where Melly lives, isn't it?' Tim asked. Cathy nodded.

'Yes, in that larch wood past Lambley road end.' She sounded pleased: Melly had always seemed as if she wanted to join in with whatever the Tates and Cubbys got up to, but somehow she had never quite made the effort.

'Great,' Tim enthused. 'Perfect hide-out. Come on, then, you lot.'

He led the way through the dark wood and behind the tip.

They crawled, single file, leaving tracks in the leafmould.

Half-way through the wood, Tim paused, with a guilty expression on his red face.

'Just remembered, I—er—I threw the key away. The shed key.... We can't put Ginger in the shed.'

'What the heck did you want to do a daft thing like that for?' Simon asked, leaning on his hands and glaring at Tim.

'Well, I dunno—it seemed like a good idea at the time—'

Duggy polished his hair gently—his head was still sore. 'Well, if we can't get into the shed, Chuck can't get out. He won't know the trick with the lock, sliding the bar out of the keep.'

'We can leave Ginger in the Land Rover.'

'Come on,' Chas said. 'It doesn't matter.'

Cathy, bringing up the rear, grinned happily. Squabble, squabble—things were back to normal again....

They found Ginger still unconscious; he moaned as they pushed him along out of the driving-seat, but even if he had tried to open his eyes they were so swollen that it would have done him no good. Cathy stared at him and shivered. Duggy sniffed.

'He's drunk, dead drunk, smell his breath.'

'No thanks,' the others chorused, disgusted.

Tim sat behind Ginger, gun in hand, just in case.

Simon drove, quite openly, up to the main road, down the new road which replaced the railway, over the river bridge and part-way up the hill at the other side, where a private road led to the Lodge. He parked off the track, then, satisfied that the Land Rover was hidden from the road, house and track in the thickly growing trees, he left Tim in charge and ran to join Cathy, Duggy and Chas. He wanted to see what kind of place this Lodge was . . . .

Melly ran down the steps to meet them, one hand grasping the collar—more like a horse-collar than anything else, Simon thought—of a tall, hungry-looking wolfhound. She appeared puzzled at the gang of grubby, tousled people on her garden path, then suddenly she recognised them.

'Hi!' she said. 'You're up early!'

Quickly Cathy explained part of what had happened, and finished by adding: 'And I wouldn't have been rescued, if you hadn't found the grip off my bike! I might have been kidnapped for ages, but for you phoning Duggy!'

Melly looked embarrassed.

'I know how fond you are of your bicycle. Didn't you say it was made in the 1940s—a collector's item?'

'Good grief,' Simon groaned. 'Collector's item? That old wreck?'

Cathy and Melly giggled and Simon groaned again. Cathy was bad enough on her own, but two of them together....

'I would tell Mum everything, I'm sure she'd want to help, but—' Melly began.

'No,' Simon snapped, turning on his heel. 'We don't want grown-ups interfering—they'll muck everything up—'

Duggy and the girls trotted after Simon, while the dog tried to wash Cathy's face. Simon was making for the garage.

'Is your car here?' he asked over his shoulder in Melly's direction.

'Well, no. My parents are away on business; that's what I was trying to tell you.'

'Why don't we leave it where it is?' Duggy suggested to Simon's back. 'The Land Rover. It's well hidden. Forget about the garage.'

'Look, why don't you all stay here till dark? From what Cathy told me, nothing much is going to happen before tomorrow. You only have to keep out of sight, if you want to catch this gang, so what could be more convenient than to stay here? You can watch television—and there's food in the freezer. Cathy and I'll go up to my room and play some new tapes, so you'll not have to be polite to me when all you want to do is doze off.'

'Polite?' Cathy thought. 'You'll be lucky.'

'You'll be dead tired by tonight if you don't sleep,' Melly went on. 'And if you have to go to Duggy's Grandad's, you'll need to be alert.' Melly gave them a mischievous grin. 'It's all so exciting.' She had, the others thought, grasped the situation rather well.

'Thanks very much,' Duggy mumbled, polishing his hair. 'It's the best idea I've heard all day—staying here, I mean. We'll mebbe just stay out here, by the Land Rover, while you lasses go inside—with yon dog.' He had interpreted Simon's frantic signals correctly. Sitting watching TV wasn't their sort of thing. They watched the girls dodging between the greening larches on their way back to the house with the dog.

Simon watched Duggy watching Melly and hummed a little tune, until Duggy noticed and turned red.

They leaned against the Land Rover, chatting to Tim. Then Duggy and Simon suddenly felt tired. Chas left them dozing in the vehicle and wandered off among the trees, thinking what a grand place this was. Lucky Melly! Then he found that the narrow gap between the larches was blocked. He drew in a sharp breath.

He was looking at a Land Rover trailer.

Meanwhile Melly was hoping that her parents wouldn't mind Cathy keeping her company; they had mentioned quite casually last week that they thought it would be better if Cathy didn't come again.

'Not quite—well, dear, they *are* village people. That curly-headed boy's language is too bad, really! I had the misfortune to hear him in the shop the other day, asking for "bullets" when he meant sweets.'

At least, Melly realised, her mother had the sense to see that if Duggy was barred Cathy wouldn't wish to be friendly. Loyalty was Cath's middle name, Melly had thought wistfully. Love me, love my friends.

She decided not to mention Cathy's visit to her parents. She wished her mother wasn't so snobbish nowadays. But it had always been the same wherever they had lived. Melly was encouraged to make friends at school, then her mother turned against them—then Melly was told that Daddy had to move, for business reasons.

Nowhere was safe, Chas now realised with dismay. Then of course, he was not certain that this was the gang's trailer. All the same, it seemed fishy, parked here, hidden. In fact, after all that had happened, he saw with a new clarity that nobody knew much about Melly's family; they had only been here a few months. Melly seemed OK, he admitted, but you never knew, ever, what people were really like until they had been tested....

Tim and Simon and Duggy, who had all curled up in the back of the Land Rover for a 'kip', as Duggy put it, were not amused at being wakened so soon.

'Sorry.' Chas did not sound sorry, 'But it's important. I think I've found the trailer that belongs to this Land Rover.'

'I'd forgotten about the trailer,' Tim whistled, tiredness forgotten. 'Anything in it?'

'Didn't look.'

Simon quirked his mouth up at one corner.

'I'll go and take a look at it,' he offered, and disappeared in the direction Chas pointed, before anybody could stop him.

He lifted the cover.

Cathy's bicycle was there—and a sack. The floor of the trailer was covered in peaty moss and fir needles.

He ran some through his fingers, kneading it as if making pastry. He picked up the sack, replaced the heavy cover and returned to the Land Rover.

'We'd better bag him,' Simon nodded towards Ginger. 'Be safer.' He climbed in beside Duggy, and in a few words explained about the trailer, while Tim and Chas struggled to pull the sack over Ginger's broad shoulders. In the absence of rope they used Tim's school tie, which spent most of its time in his anorak pocket, to secure the bottom of the bag.

'What now?' Simon enquired, settling against the side of the Rover.

'Well, I doubt if Melly's folk would leave her here if there was any fear of the gang coming—I'm willing to bet that her folks are mixed up in this.... I just hope Melly isn't, 'cos Cathy'll have told her everything that's happened.'

'You reckon this is the gang's headquarters, Chas?' Duggy asked.

Chas shrugged. 'Could be—'

'They'll never think of looking for us here,' Tim chortled. He patted the Land Rover. 'This is our Trojan Horse, in a way.'

'We'll wait till it's the darkening, then have a look round the house—see if there's anything funny going on, raid their freezer, then we'll be on our way up-by to Alston, to see Duggy's Grandad. He'll know what we should do.'

So it was agreed that Simon's was the best plan. They had no idea where the rest of the gang was, but the action seemed, according to the conversation between Chuck and the unknown man in old Bas's shed, to be moving to Haltwhistle in the morning. Nine for ten....

'We've got great faith in Duggy's Grandad,' Chas agreed. 'He's the right man to tell us what we should do. Simon's right—this time.'

'I think the gang's too well organised—too ruthless,' Tim said. 'I mean, I know that Unicus is important—bound to be. But you wouldn't think it would be worth all this bother—kidnapping us and all that. I mean, this gang seems to have loads of members in it—they'll all be to pay. And how much would they get for a set of plans for a— a—' he searched for a phrase which would not upset Duggy. 'Well, after all, it *is* just a steam engine, isn't it? We got rid of most of them years ago, so who's likely to want to start making them again? All that tooling up and everything.'

The phrase did upset Duggy, but he felt quite sorry for them for not knowing exactly what Unicus was.

He explained: 'OK—I'd better tell you.' He gave a quick polish to his hair. 'Unicus—the whole loco is different from anything there's ever been before. She's sort of torpedo-shaped, stable, fast, safe and'—he looked round his audience—'she's powered by batteries—solar batteries.'

'Ah, yes,' Chas breathed. 'They've been trying to do that for years.'

'Not like this, they haven't. One initial charge from the mains, and after that they'll be self-charging, partly from solar energy, and partly from the special ceramic they're encased in. Unused power isn't wasted—it's sent round and round the ceramic till it's needed to boost the batteries. Then the power builds up again, and that's stored in the ceramic body—perpetual power, you might say—perpetual regenerating power, anyway. And she doesn't look like a loco, more like a space-shuttle with flanged wheels—ceramic wheels. One of the best things about this stuff is that it's made in local foundries. Like steel, it's fired to a tremendous heat—I forget the exact temperature, but it would make your hair stand on end—then cast, like steel. The drawback of ordinary ceramic is that when you fire anything big, it distorts in the kiln, but this stuff of Dad's can be cast, like I said. And this is the exciting bit—the minerals are from this area.

'You know how Dad's always been one for ratching about the moors. Well one day he came across some chunks of glassy stone, buried in what he thought was a Celtic site—a local historian reckoned it was Celtic, because of the tools and jewelry and stuff they found nearby. Dad read up about Celts and he discovered that archaeologists in Italy, I think—or France mebbe —anyway, they found a smelter that proved that the Celts had discovered a fuel, or a way of using charcoal, that was far hotter than the ordinary charcoal that scientists had thought they used. They found primitive batteries, as well.... They used to think that the Celts had spread their discoveries and inventions as they came west, but now they think there was a kind of simultaneous discovery. So Dad reckoned that our Celts must've found the stuff, on

Alston Moor. Well they would—wouldn't they? They were clever—they would use what there was—local stuff.

'Well, it was the spring after the big snowstorm, and there was water everywhere—great floods that opened up the fells like hushes, so that you could see different layers of rocks that were buried before, and 'cos you're not allowed to dig at these old sites, they wouldn't have been discovered at all, but for the storms. Dad had some of the rock analysed, and it was the same as the chunks of glassy stuff he'd found at the Celtic site—some sort of burial chamber, it was. One thing led to another, and mind, this took him years. I mean, that big snowstorm was in 1963. That'll give you some idea—he's just got everything together now after all these years.... And that's about all.'

Suddenly embarrassed at his own enthusiasm, Duggy touched up his hair, yet again, and gazed down at his feet. Cathy and Melly had crept up, unnoticed, and were listening, enthralled, at the open side-window.

'Gosh,' Cathy sighed. 'Imagine; what happened, d'ye think, to the men of Alston Moor—our ancestors. What became of them?'

'They buried their valuables and scarpered before the Romans found 'em,' Duggy said. 'They were survivors.'

Nobody contradicted him.

'Well, I can see now why everybody's excited about Unicus—apart from the historic bit, I mean.' Tim leaned back in his seat until it creaked. 'Fancy your Dad doing all that research.' He looked at Duggy, curiosity and politeness battling; curiosity won. 'You wouldn't think he would be interested in that sort of thing—science and history, archaeology.'

Duggy struggled to control his temper and failed.

'You mean you think he's too thick, just 'cos he's an engine-driver? He gets his hands dirty, like me, but that doesn't turn us into morons, does it? Or you think you're better than we are, just because your Dad works in an office or something. He's not even a proper farmer—he just plays at it....'

Tim flushed. 'Oh—come on, Duggy, you know I didn't mean that. All I said was—'

'Oh, shut up, the pair of you! Just shut up!' Cathy broke in. 'You've gone and spoiled it all now. I was just thinking how lovely it would be if we could go back in time, and see what it was really like. You know, real people, not just words in a history book—but you have to spoil it.'

'I know,' Melly poured oil tentatively. 'Like *Puck of Pook's Hill*—'

They all chorused: 'Oak, ash and thorn.... '

'Try a bit of rowan, too,' Chas suggested. 'You never know what'll happen with rowan.'

'There's something magic about being in a wood, like this—you'd expect to see Celts and Druids and things living somewhere like this,' Cathy said dreamily, her eyes staring blankly, as if the past was inside her head.

'I didn't know you were into the occult,' Simon said.

'Lot of rubbish that is; we shouldn't be talking about it, not even in fun,' Chas declared.

'That's right—it *is* rubbish,' Simon agreed.

'You've forgotten!' Cathy exclaimed. 'You've forgotten that time when we went—'

'That's enough,' Simon snapped, with a warning glance at Cathy. They both remembered a visit to Long Meg stone circle one summer night.

Duggy and Tim sat silent, simmering.

Duggy never really had the same regard for Tim, after that day.

And Tim knew it.

'Aye, that's more than enough,' Duggy said. 'I dunno what we've got on to, but we have a job to do and I think we should be thinking about that, instead of niggling each other.'

Tim thumped Duggy's shoulder and they both grinned, patching up the quarrel. But it was a large hole; it needed a large patch.

'Some people will not be chuffed about Unicus.' Chas's voice was sombre. 'Such as steel firms—especially if this new stuff lasts as long as you reckon, Duggy.'

'There'd be some folk definitely unchuffed when the cog-wheel was invented, but it still caught on,' Tim said.

'Well, it's bound to have something against it—every new invention has. But from what Duggy says, it seems OK—I can't see anything wrong with it, offhand.' Simon admitted. 'Sounds as if it's totally impervious to everything . . . I suppose it'll have been tested and everything—else they wouldn't be allowing it on the railway to carry passengers.'

Duggy nodded, gratified by what he considered to be a long overdue interest in Unicus.

'The only snag is that it's so hard—the ceramic, I mean—that everything has to be added into the pattern at the start. You can't add bits on to the casting afterwards, or screw bits on, unless the screw thread is moulded as part of the casting. But you can join two pieces of ceramic just by using a thin layer of molten ceramic—the way they use slip on pottery. And it won't rust, or need painting.'

'Sounds marvellous,' Cathy agreed. 'But it's getting late—and all we've done so far is talk, eat and sleep.'

'And tomorrow's Monday.' Melly did a little dance on the grass. 'May Day! Wake me early, Mother dear, for I'm to be Queen of the May, Mother.'

She laughed as the boys stared at her.

'You're as daft as she is!' Simon commented, with a nod in Cathy's direction.

Duggy pulled himself together and continued: 'Remember that Dad phoned and said to go to Alston—to Grandad's?

Well, we've got to get to Alston first. So, what about trying the railmotor again, Si, see if it'll start?'

'What about the carb? I mean, don't expect too much.... If it was muck in the carburettor that gummed it up, it'll still be there—it will have settled, but it's bound to get stirred up when we start the engine—especially if there's not much petrol in the tank and possibly dirt in there as well and it'll be nearly empty, I suppose.'

'You mean if we had some more petrol to put in, we wouldn't have any more bother?' Duggy asked.

'Well, if it's the suction pipe in the tank that's bunged with dirt, or rust—which it probably is—we stand a better chance of getting to Alston with more juice in the tank. More petrol in the tank won't slosh about so much and churn all the dirt up to the outlet pipe. In fact, we may just have run out of petrol.' Simon was cautious.

'We have another problem, then. No garage between Halt-whistle and Alston,' Tim said, with something like his old spirit. 'But are we not at this very moment sitting in a Land Rover with petrol lapping over its filler-cap?'

Simon shook his head. 'No, it's a diesel engine.'

'I'll get some for you! Dad always keeps a few spare cans in the garage, in case he's ever stuck,' Melly said.

'Good lass,' Duggy said, forgetting his shyness, or whatever it was. 'That'll be grand—if only the railmotor works—'

But Melly was already on her way through the trees.

'What I want to know is: why have we got to go to Duggy's Grandad's?' Cathy asked, watching her friend's graceful exit and wishing she was as tall and slim as Melly. 'I've been wondering why we've got to take the risk. The place'll be crawling with policemen and visitors, as well as people we know. We're bound to be recognised. And if we're driving up to Alston in this Land Rover—well, it's asking for trouble. They'll be stopping all vehicles going into the town—they always do when somebody's kidnapped. You see them on TV. We could stay here till morning, then go up, if we've got to—but nobody's told me why we absolutely must go to old Duggy's place....'

Duggy gave her a disparaging look. 'Because Dad said I had to, that's why. He phoned especially, so it must be pretty important. Actually, I think it's to make sure that Grandad doesn't sleep in. You see, Dad'll be driving Unicus tomorrow, and Grandad'll be driving the Daler. The Daler's hauling the observation coaches from Alston to Haltwhistle for a grand opening there, picking up the VIPs there and running them back to Alston for the main celebrations. They've laid on a special do in the café—South Tyne salmon, Alston Moor lamb, you know the sort of thing—that's why Mum's stayed at Alston. And that's why she's been like a hen on a hot girdle these past few weeks.

'The VIPs—most of them—will be travelling to Haltwhistle on the main line from Carlisle, so the Daler has to be at Haltwhistle in good time. The idea is to let the Daler be the main attraction, then Dad'll follow down quietly in his Unicus. The old and the new together—a sort of—what d'ye call it? You know, a look backwards and forwards at the same time.

'I just hope Dad makes it—dunno where he can be—but he did phone, so he's OK. Let's hope Unicus is safe in yon old shed at Alston. Anybody could cart Unicus away in a low-loader, if they really wanted her. I've been thinking about that—wouldn't put it past the gang to try, if nothing happens about us tomorrow after the deadline for swapping us for Unicus. I just don't know what's going to happen when they find out they haven't got us—they'll be desperate by then. Here! I hope they don't try anything with Dad—or Grandad!'

'Don't worry, man,' Simon told him. 'We'll give ourselves

up to the gang if they threaten our families. It will be interesting, though, seeing what the gang does in the end.'

'The whole gang'll probably turn up at Lambley station—they'll imagine we're still in old Bas's shed—and they'll plan on doing something drastic to us. Just as well we're not there,' Cathy said, with a shiver of genuine fear. 'I can still see the expression in their eyes.'

'Well, all I know is that the Alston Line has to be opened properly. Ten prompt tomorrow. They buried the line in 1976 with wreaths—we'll open it with bouquets, like Mum said.' Duggy said, with a touch of poetry. 'The Daler'll show them what a proper engine's like. I wonder if we have to help Grandad with the engine. He's getting on a bit—been retired for years, so he'll be a bit rusty. I could offer to do a bit of firing or even driving.—' Duggy's first loyalty was to steam, proud though he was of Unicus and all it stood for. Tomorrow was his big day. Gang or no gang, he was going to enjoy it.

'I think your Dad's got Unicus stashed away somewhere—I don't think it's at Alston at all. Too obvious—the gang could tow it away on a lorry. I mean, if anybody put their mind to it, they could break into those sheds.' Tim said.

'And there's another thing.' Tim spoke quickly, almost gabbling in his haste to put his ideas into words. 'If Unicus is at Alston—and as far as the gang knows—it is at Alston—then why have they put it about that we are somewhere on Alston Moor? They will know that the police will be looking for us up there, and pinching Unicus would be pretty conspicuous, they'd never get away with it. If they really want the new loco, they could just as easily have put it about that they had us locked up somewhere round Haltwhistle—or anywhere—just to draw attention away from where the action's going to be, that is, Alston, if they're to be believed, which they're not. We know for a fact that the gang's going to Haltwhistle. Just the opposite—they've deliberately diverted attention to Alston.'

Melly appeared in the silence following Tim's remarks, struggling with the gallon can. Duggy jogged over to take it from her, setting it down on the grass with a suddenness which set the petrol slurping inside, against the plastic. He stood, staring at it, until Tim spoke again.

'It all seems so logical, you know: kidnappers exchanging son of inventor for blueprints and prototype loco. But it isn't the usual thing, is it? I mean, usually hijackers want money, or a plane to fly them off somewhere, or else they want prisoners released. But this is different. Big Duggy probably has the plans in his head. He could build another loco, make the ceramic again. And even if the gang got hold of the plans, or the loco, and sold them—well, I mean, everybody'd know who they really belong to. It's not like stealing plans for a new weapon—the gang could use that to blackmail governments with. But a loco! Even the new ceramic takes a bit of swallowing! Yes, it *is* brilliant and all that, but is it brilliant enough? Well, is it?' He looked round the silent circle. 'Well?'

'There's big money to be made in industry,' Chas said slowly. 'But I know what you are getting at.'

'Industrial sabotage—that's what Simon thought you were worried about, Duggy! Remember, Si? The day we saw the red Range Rover outside the Post Office and Duggy went off in a huff 'cos I mentioned his Dad's new loco?'

'Calm down, Cath,' Simon muttered, embarrassed. 'I remember all right.'

'Well, I dunno. | It could be a double bluff, mebbe, but it was a bit funny, Dad going off like that—not telling Mum and me where he was going to be. But if it's not Unicus they're after, then what?'

'We've been set up!' Chas announced. 'We've been taken for a bunch of idiots. We *are* a bunch of idiots for not seeing it before.'

'What—how d'ye mean, Chas?' Cathy asked nervously, glancing round at the encroaching dusk. Trees which had seemed safe—sheltering—now loomed threateningly. She had always thought that larches were like elegant ladies, dripping with lace; now she saw that they were faceless things, with ragged clothes....

'Well, something's been at the back of my mind ever since Duggy bragged about all those VIPs who are coming for the opening—but I couldn't put a finger on it till now.'

'Aye,' Simon admitted. 'I did wonder why the gang flaunted a new red Range Rover—a stolen one at that, according to the radio. I mean, nobody who wants to be surreptitious goes round in one of those—not in a country place like this, where everybody knows what everybody else drives. Then we were carted off in a Land Rover. That I can understand—a Land Rover is as good as camouflage round here. All the farmers seem to drive one—one extra wouldn't be noticed. The Range Rover must've been a sort of decoy. The gang wanted to be noticed at Alston—they wanted the police to be up at Alston from the beginning. Well, what're we waiting for? And what about him?' He gestured at Ginger. 'Still out for the count. He must be soaked in whisky or whatever it is.'

'Aye—and the bee-stings'll not have helped,' Duggy said thoughtfully. They all heard him take in a great gulp of air, then he said excitedly: 'Listen. We've got to get Grandad to take the Daler to Haltwhistle tonight. The gang'll expect it going down in the morning—ALPS have timetables all over the place. They'll expect it leaving Alston on time tomorrow. If we take her tonight, we'll have time to do a recce round Haltwhistle, and nobody any wiser. Nobody'll ever think we're down there—and don't forget, we're the only ones who've seen the gang in action and we know all the short cuts and lonnens in Haltwhistle—I'll bet we can track that lot down between us. If we wait till the morning the police'll be about—always are, when there's important folk coming. They'll be stopping cars, but they'll never think of us turning up in a loco tonight!'

'Please,' Cathy murmured. 'Will somebody please tell me what's going on? Everybody seems to know, except me.'

'Assassination! That's what we're on about. We reckon the gang's going to knock off a politician or mebbe all of the politicians and all those people who are turning up at the railway opening. I say,' Simon added soberly, 'they'll be sitting ducks.'

'But why should they want—?' Cathy began.

'Use your head, Cath!' Simon broke in impatiently: 'People are always wanting to kill politicians—and the Home Secretary's coming tomorrow, and the Minister for the Environment and a lot more. Duggy's told you, so just shut up.'

Duggy stirred the spanners in his boiler-suit pockets.

'If I can find the key for the points, we'll be away, and see if we can start the railmotor. It's got to work. If it doesn't, it'll take us half the night to walk to Alston.' The key surfaced and he handed it to Simon. 'Here you are—you know what to do, you'll need it at Alston. We'll have more help this time.' Mebbe too much, he thought; it would be a crush with all this lot on board.

'Just hope we're not stopped on the way back from here to Lambley,' Chas put in, only to be squashed by Tim telling him not to be such a wet blanket.

Duggy was ahead of the rest of them, planning where to leave the Daler once they got it down to Haltwhistle. 'We want it out of sight. The Plenmellor sidings'll be the best place—near enough to Haltwhistle, yet away from the road. And the factories are closed for the May Day holiday, so there'll be nobody snooping about.'

'Why can't you and old Duggy take the loco down, and the

rest of us go to Haltwhistle in this Land Rover?' Cathy asked. She was, in the end, scared of riding on the railmotor. And the Daler, she thought, would be worse—like a great monster.

'And get arrested? Not likely. Too risky, anyway. We know the gang's down there at Haltwhistle—that's why we're going. They'd recognise their own Land Rover, wouldn't they?' Simon felt that he had done little else but snub Cathy all weekend, but honestly, he thought, exasperated; honestly. At the back of his mind he knew why he was so edgy these days; he felt guilty at letting the family down by turning against farming. It seemed to him to mean years and years of seven-day-a-week toil and what did you have at the end?

Tim climbed into the driving-seat, checked that Ginger was still secure, and leaned out of the window. 'Room inside, Melly! Hop in.'

'Well,' Melly hesitated.

'You're too well-behaved to come with the likes of us.' Cathy joked. 'You don't have to, you know—but you'll be sorry if you miss this great rescue bid by Slaggyford teenagers.'

Melly had climbed into the back before Cathy had finished.

'Your folks'll know you're with us, or with me anyway,' Cathy said, reflecting that Melly seemed to lead a pretty boring life. 'If they come back early.'

'That's what's worrying Melly,' Chas murmured.

'What about Tiny?' Cathy gasped suddenly, grabbing Melly's arm.

'What about who?' Simon asked

'The dog—you know—' Cathy said.

'Ah—*that* Tiny—well, he can't come with us—there's not room, and he'll bark....'

'Oh—he'll be OK,' Melly said carelessly. 'He's used to being left—he'll look after the house.'

'Good. I can't stand big dogs—they always want to wash your face.' Tim, hampered by Ginger lolling in the passenger seat, let in the clutch and eased off the grass and on to the rutted track leading to the main road.

'Well, what's wrong with that?' Melly thought a wash of any sort wouldn't come amiss as far as any of them were concerned.

Tim glanced in the rear-view mirror to watch Melly's face as he said: 'Well, think about where he's likely to have washed before he gets round to your face.' He grinned.

Good job it wasn't far to Lambley station. He changed down to a lower gear to take the steep hill up to the Brampton–Alston road junction. There was no other traffic. He grinned again, wondering what the folk from the cottage would think of Duggy's appearance and disappearance, and the mess they'd left—and they'd forgotten to leave a note. They would have to remember to pay for the food. It was much lighter, away from the trees; the moon would be up soon. He was looking forward to the railmotor trip, and the steam loco should be quite exciting—it was the bit after that which worried him. He hadn't meant to be rude about Duggy's Dad, but Duggy always seemed to pick things up the wrong way.

Duggy droned on behind, about the loco.

'It'll take mebbe four hours to get up steam,' he was saying. 'By the time we get up to Alston, fetch Grandad and get the loco boiler up to pressure, it'll be about twelveish—so we'll have plenty of time to find out what's going on with the gang. It'll be great going with a proper loco on the Alston line.'

'The Midnight Line,' Cathy whispered, but nobody heard.

13

Duggy's life was trains; nothing else had ever mattered. This, he felt, was the greatest night of his life.

'Better keep quiet about all this—afterwards, I mean,' he said 'We're breaking all sorts of laws and rules. Let's hope—' He was about to say: 'Let's hope it won't affect my chances of training to be a BR driver', but he remembered in time that he had not mentioned anything about leaving school this summer to start training to be a loco driver. That news would keep for some other time.

Aloud, he said: 'We'll park the railmotor this side of Alston station. That way nobody'll hear the row—not that there'll be anybody about on the sidings at this time of night, and they'll not expect us. Grandad's going to be surprised when we want him to turn out tonight.'

'That's the snag, isn't it, Duggy? Having to walk up to your Grandad's house, I mean. There'll be folk about in the town. Somebody might recognise you—even if the street lights aren't all that brilliant. Your family's notorious now, one way or another—' Chas paused, then went on resolutely: 'I'll go and fetch Old Duggy down to the engine sheds, if you like. Nobody'll recognise me—not on my own—but they might be suspicious if we all turn out. Your Grandad lives down The Butts, doesn't he?'

Simon threw back his head and laughed. 'What? Go on—not recognise you? You might as well hire the band.'

'We'll have to disguise you—put your hair off your face, inside your anorak hood, like this.' Cathy demonstrated with her own hood. 'And walk differently—don't just skulk about with your hands in your pockets like you generally do. That makes you look shifty, for a start, as if you're pretending you're not here.' She was suddenly inspired. 'I know! I'll come with you and we'll pretend to be a courting couple!'

'Pretend?' Tim murmured with a sly glance in the mirror at Chas, this time. Chas blushed furiously.

'Well—' Chas sounded as if an elephant was sitting on his chest.

'That's settled then,' Cathy said. 'I say, Duggy, isn't it a bit confusing for your family—with three generations all called Duggy? Oh, we're here already.'

The Land Rover coasted down into Lambley station, fetching up at the platform near old Bas's shed.

'That'll do, Tim,' Simon yelled. 'Any closer and we'll not get the door open. Pity about the shed key—what the heck you chucked it away for—'

''Cos I'm not as clever as you are, I suppose!'

'Tim—Simon—give over, will you? Stop bickering. Listen— I dunno if it was that knock on the head or what, but I've just remembered something important—'

They stood on the platform, waiting for Duggy to explain. Cathy moved as far as she could, from the shed; the memory of being in there, in that sack, made her feel sick.

Tim locked the Land Rover and pocketed the key with a meaningful glance at Simon, who noticed it. But he too, had remembered something.

'The viaduct!' He sounded fed up. 'Just before that cretin hit me with a spanner, Duggy and I noticed a sort of silvery wire shining on the viaduct wall. We were just going to investigate it when they mugged us.'

As one man, they turned and ran, past the orchard and on

to the bridge. A hundred and ten feet below, the South Tyne squeezed between the arches and roared down over the rocky valley floor. As always, Cathy breathed in deeply, to lessen the weight on the viaduct; they all did, in case something disastrous happened if they did not. Old as they were, they still avoided cracks in pavements too, just in case.

Duggy deviated, having caught sight of the beehive scattered over the orchard; glad of the dusk, he piled the lifts on to the base of the hive—gently—and put the roof on top. There was nothing he could do about the broken frames and wax. The bees were clustered round the queen and took little notice as he rebuilt the hive over their heads.

Bas'll go spare when he sees that lot, Duggy thought, as he rejoined the others on the viaduct.

'Listen,' he panted. 'I think one of us should keep an eye on the orchard end of the bridge and one on the north end as well; we don't want to be caught in the middle with nowhere to go, if some of the gang come back.'

'I'll go,' the twins volunteered, and Tim took the orchard while Chas crouched behind some willow bushes at the far end.

'Right. Heads down and mouths shut.' Duggy had taken charge. Nobody objected.

Suddenly they were aware of what might happen . . .

'I'm really scared,' Cathy whispered in Melly's ear. 'Isn't it grand?'

Melly was equally scared, but less enthusiastic; she merely nodded and rubbed her ear.

Duggy crept along in the shadow of the wall, keeping to the grassed verge—away from the crunchy newly-laid ballast.

Following him, Simon felt a familiar cringe of fear as he came to the start of the viaduct and realised that it was 110 feet above that narrow, twisting, silver ribbon that was the South Tyne. He felt that if he looked over the parapet he would overbalance, so he kept his head down, searching for the wire which had attracted their attention earlier. At first it seemed as if it had gone, and Simon felt relief welling up inside—then Duggy nudged him and pointed.

They knelt down and traced the length of the wire running along the sleepers, almost covered by the ballast. Once they knew where to look, it was easy to find the rest.

It stretched across the straight middle section and round the curve at the Haltwhistle end, then it went over the lineside wall and disappeared in the undergrowth near where Chas lurked.

Simon and the girls stared at the wire, then at Duggy, who shook his head and squatted on his hunkers.

'Shot wire,' he breathed in Simon's ear. 'We've got to find what's at the other end . . .'

Scarcely breathing, they scuttled back to retrace the wire, where it ran down into what they now saw was a manhole cover, covered with a thick layer of ballast. Like a couple of

eager terriers after a rabbit, they raked the ballast away and
lifted the heavy manhole cover.

Cathy and Melly watched, fascinated. 'What's in there?'
Cathy whispered

'Looks like geli!' Duggy whispered back.

'What?'

'Shush!'

Suddenly Simon had a mental picture of Duggy and himself
creeping about, uncovering a manhole full of jelly. He felt a
great laugh building up and, in spite of deep breathing and
tightening of stomach muscles, a muffled snort escaped him.
Cathy caught his agonised glance and understood the joke.
They both crouched on all fours, shaking with almost-silent
laughter.

'Give over, you idiots!' Duggy hissed. Leaning on his hands,
he glared at them. 'Will you stop your row or d'ye want us all
blown up? This isn't a game, you know—there could be
enough geli in here to blow umpteen viaducts up.' And he
added: 'And us.... '

'Sorry, Dug. Dunno what came over us,' Simon apologised,
then spoiled it by snorting again. 'What'll we do about it? The
explosive, I mean.' He registered that the pressure was getting to them all. Still, Duggy had a good right to be ratty: he
was the only one able to cope with the gelignite. Come to
think of it, he could cope with all sorts of things; he had an
uncle in mining, who would have told him about geli. That
took guts, knowing the risks and getting on with the job, while
Cath and himself fell about laughing. Still, it had seemed
funny.

'Aye,' Duggy whispered. 'We'd better look for another wire
in case they've planted two—try along the other side of the
sleepers yonder.'

There *was* another wire. Shorter than the first one, it led
from a manhole at the Haltwhistle end of the viaduct, trailed

under the ballast and finished up in the wood, running parallel with the first wire. Duggy snipped a few feet of wire from each length and pocketed it, then they reburied the loose ends in the ballast, smoothing away all signs of their burrowing operations. Then they signalled to the Cubbys to return to the station house.

'Time for a confab,' Duggy whispered.

They sat in the darkening kitchen. Cathy stared down the line. 'Just in case,' she told Melly, who immediately looked scared and backed away from the window.

Noticing Melly's reaction, Tim reassured her: 'They'll be long gone. Whoever planted that geli, they wouldn't hang about—wouldn't you say, Duggy?'

Duggy nodded. 'Aye—if they've any sense. But I've been thinking about that..They could've planned on blowing more bridges, for all we know. We'll never be able to check the lot.'

'Why?' Cathy asked. 'I mean, why do they want to go about blowing bridges up? And you—' She turned to Duggy. 'Why couldn't you have told me it was gelignite in that manhole? You and your jelly.'

'Just you watch the platform and never mind him and his jelly,' Simon told her, conveniently forgetting that he had started the giggling fit. 'We've got to get things straight before we go any further!' He glanced round the room. 'Right?'

'We should all say what we think's going on, and what we should do about it—you start, eh, Simon?' Tim suggested; 'It's your idea.' He put his hands together and rested his chin on the apex, leaning back until his chair squeaked.

Simon checked on his fingers as he spoke slowly: 'One, I reckon that Tim should pay for that chair when it collapses—we're in enough debt as it is, what with one thing and another. Two, judging from the way the gang snapped us up in the first place—they must've kept tabs on us for a long time. They knew exactly where we were going on Saturday.

They knew where Cathy was—they planned on kidnapping her on Kirkhaugh bank. Three, they knew where Tim and Chas were. That Land Rover was parked at the lime-hopper level-crossing, waiting. Now, how the heck did they know where we were going to be, when we hardly knew ourselves? I mean, it was just a fluke that we didn't all keep together instead of separating and going off in different directions. So how did they know?'

Cathy's shoulders rose as she shivered; she turned to look at Simon, and in a low, scared voice said: 'They've been watching us all the time, haven't they? They must have had radios or something, to keep in touch....' She shivered again. 'Si, I feel all sort of creepy—I hate being watched.'

Ignoring his sister's creepiness, Simon tapped his right thumb-nail against his two front teeth.

'Something must've gone wrong. They missed seeing which way me and Duggy went. They wouldn't bargain on us leaving the road—and Cath—and going along the railway. So, that's the point when they stopped watching us—when they thought they could pick us up on the road. They would see us setting off, I suppose. At a guess, I'd say that, except for Ginger and Chuck, who had to stay to keep an eye on us, they all pushed off when they thought they had us all sewn up. But the men in the Range Rover probably had other things to do—like sticking geli in the viaduct, for instance. We saw them set off down the line, from Alston station, rucksacks and all. Imagine we're tied up in the shed and Duggy in here, also tied up, and there the gang is: gone. The police are searching for us on Alston Moor. And those VIPs are making towards Haltwhistle to be knocked off by the gang. As Chas said, we've been set up. All that the gang really wants is blood money. We're certainly in trouble this time.'

Melly drew in a deep breath; she remembered that her mother had told her not to mingle with the village children.

She also remembered that her parents always phoned to check that she was all right when they were away overnight. Melly made up her mind to go home as soon as she could after this rail trip.

Chas looked down at the foot he was waggling.

'So, blowing up a bridge or two will be no more than a ploy to distract attention from Haltwhistle—probably to give the gang time to escape after the assassination.'

'Sounds feasible,' Simon agreed. 'Well, if that's the case, they'll blow them up after ten o'clock and not before. Blown before that time, and this place would be swarming with police, and the gang won't want that—not with us locked in yonder shed, as they believe. They'll want the law up here after they've done their murders, so's they can make a neat get-away from Haltwhistle. Hey!' Simon sat up straight. 'There was a lot of explosive packed into that manhole—not that I know much about it—and old Basil's shed isn't that far from the viaduct!'

Tim whistled.

'Time to go, lads and lasses.' He stood up. 'It's dark enough now—we can push the railmotor along the line, out of earshot of that farmhouse down the field, then start the engine, with a bit of luck and that extra petrol.' He sat down again, suddenly and almost fatally, as far as the chair was concerned. 'Supposing we're right about them blowing up the viaduct tomorrow—who's going to press the button? Somebody must be hanging about, waiting.... I mean—there's no way they can do it by some sort of remote control, is there?'

Duggy shook his head.

'Well, they can't blow it now. I've snipped the wires—no need to panic.'

'I know that, man. But *they* don't. The gang'll think every-thing's the way they left it—including us—and the shot wire. If they had remote control, they wouldn't have needed the long wires to fire the charges with a hand exploder, so they must have somebody planted here,' Tim gabbled excitedly. 'And where else? Will it be safe to drive the Daler from Alston tonight? They've had time to plant geli under all the bridges. We can't risk it! We can't risk your Grandad, Duggy,—never mind us—and the loco. And we can't inspect every bridge on the Alston line. How many are there? Thirty-odd? It's just not on.' He combed his hair back with his fingers.

'Oh, come on. They only want to distract attention—not flatten the entire South Tyne valley. Once they've done the deed, they'll just want to escape—and it'll be easier for them if the police are decoyed up here, investigating the explosion, instead of at Haltwhistle, investigating the massacre. If we've got it right, it's an extremely crafty plot, when you consider,' Chas said. 'You can see Lambley from a long way off.'

'Aye, the hill at the east end of the viaduct, what the railway navvies left of it, was one of the ancient watch places—part of a chain: Whitley Castle, Lintley, Lambley and Haltwhistle, and there's the Castle Hill and Carvoran. They would have had bonfires ready to light, if the Armada had got off the ground—if you see what I mean!' Simon added hastily.

'How did they expect the Armada to get this far up the Tyne?' Cathy couldn't resist joking, but the only reaction was a black look from Simon and a mumbled 'History. Huh!' from Tim.

'I don't understand how you can sit there and just niggle away at each other, when all this is going on—kidnapping and things,' Melly said.

'What we're doing is not niggling, dear girl. We are having a frank and amiable exchange of ideas.' Tim said.

'I just hope I'm not here when you start niggling.'

'What's it got -' Simon began, forgetting for a moment that Melly was well brought up. He omitted to add: 'to do with you.' But Cathy heard him distinctly not saying it, and grinned. Simon being tactful. Well, well.

In spite of their jokey attitude, they all knew that this was the worst, the most dangerous situation they had ever had to face.

'I still don't see why we can't just drive up to Alston in the Land Rover, ' Cathy began.

'We've been through all that before—you should listen to what's going on, instead of dreaming!' Simon snapped.

Duggy interrupted him: 'I think you're all wrong. About the gang murdering all those folks at Haltwhistle. I think they're out to stop Unicus being launched—one way or another. If they can't have it, they'll stop anybody else from having it. And they'll keep on blowing things up till we get fed up and let them have it. Why else did they say I was their trump card? It must be something to do with the loco—the ceramics. It's got to be,' he added obstinately.

'Perhaps they're terrorists practising on the Alston Line, before promoting themselves to blowing up an airport, or London Bridge,' Melly said. 'Anyway, it's as sensible as your theories. You're all guessing. You don't know anything, really.'

'You can say that again,' Simon murmured. 'And anyway, you're the one that wanted to come with us, not five minutes ago.'

'Well, yes, I did. But I've had time to think, and it's all a bit far-fetched, isn't it? From what Cathy told me earlier, the gang probably locked you up to teach you a lesson for being so cheeky!'

Simon prepared to wade in, but Cathy shouted: 'Stop it!'

'Cathy's right. This is no time to fall out—let's go and stop the Haltwhistle massacre,' Tim said. 'At least we know where we stand now.' He added to himself: 'Except for Melly and her folk.'

'Let's go and save Unicus!' Duggy snorted. 'I'll carry the petrol can.'

'Better cut along by the wood and the tip, as before,' Tim suggested, leading the way over the fence and into the wood. 'It's really weird, there's nobody about, yet you feel there might be somebody lurking.'

Minutes later the railmotor was pushed out of the sand drag, over the points and along the track for a hundred yards or so southwards.

'Surely nobody's going to hear the engine running at this distance from Lambley,' Duggy puffed. 'Feels as if we've pushed this for a mile. We'll fill her up and try it.'

The engine chuntered into life. Duggy beamed.

Tim leaped on board, turned and said,' Any more for the *Skylark?'*

Duggy concentrated on keeping his speed down, so that the engine ran with slightly less noise than before, and also used less petrol. It was tempting, though, to frighten the girls by opening the throttle; but he resisted.

Cathy and Melly hung on, their eyes shining with mingled pleasure and fear as they trundled along the valley.

They kept a sharp lookout for shot wire.

Duggy felt uneasy when Slaggyford level-crossing came in sight. What if a car came up the road when they were on the crossing? If he stopped the railmotor it might not start again. He glanced at Simon, but he seemed engrossed in something or other.

Suddenly car lights veered off the main road and turned up the station bank. Duggy saw the lights judder slightly as the car driver changed gear. His mouth was open to shout a warning to the others. Car and railmotor were converging; it was too late to stop; they were on a collision course. He imagined metal slicing through metal....

Then the beams curved again, winking as they passed the beech hedge surrounding the bungalow below the crossing, before disappearing into the garage.

'D'ye know I could swear there was something on the railway just now—just caught a glimpse. Must be some sort of mental thingummy—prescience,' the car driver told his wife as they sat down to dinner.

It was some time afterwards when the full horror of what could have happened hit the others, but Duggy knew at the time how close they had been to a messy accident.

Duggy realised that it was too much for them; they needed help. He worried at the problem for the rest of the journey.

Moonlight glanced off the higgledy-piggledy rooftops of Alston, the bland modern school and, down in the valley, the long row of station buildings. Duggy reduced the engine speed and the railmotor came to a gentle halt. Simon set the points and Duggy drove into the siding.

'Great,' Duggy whispered, polishing his hair furiously.

'Now for the difficult bit,' Tim observed, glancing at Cathy.

'What? Oh, yes. We're going to collect Duggy's Grandad, aren't we?' Cathy nodded; she linked her arm in that of a brilliantly blushing Chas, whose light was, however, hidden behind a bushel of wavy hair.

'Now, remember what I said,' Cathy said briskly. 'Different walk, hair inside hood—well, go on then. Tuck it inside. And shoulders back. Purposeful, that's what we want to seem. See you lot later—we'll bring Mr. Stevens back . . . you will look out for us, won't you? No need to stay rooted to the spot but don't disappear either. Your Grandad's going to be surprised, isn't he, Dug? I just hope he recognises us.'

Duggy's teeth gleamed in the moonlight as he grinned and nodded.

'Don't forget to tell him to bring the loco-shed keys—his memory's not what it was.'

Pausing only to wave to a forlorn Melly, Cathy dragged Chas by his sleeve and they scuttled along the line, taking a wide detour to avoid passing the station buildings, in case they were recognised. They squeezed along beside the wall where, surprisingly, the Range Rover still stood. Lights blazed in the buildings and in the house; but nobody noticed them moving in the shadows. Once on the main road, they ceased skulking; they turned up the steep stone steps to the back lane leading to The Butts, where small, deep-set windows seemed to frown on them on either hand.

A black cat, almost invisible except for its green eyes, slunk behind them, stopping when they stopped, rubbing against Cathy's ankles as if it had known her for years.

'This is it,' Cathy whispered, stopping suddenly. 'No lights on—he must be in bed.'

They stared at the heavy panelled door. Cathy was reaching for the knocker when, from behind the door, a dog barked. It was the bark of a large, alert dog. A light went on upstairs, then they heard a sash window sliding open. The cat bolted.

'What's up?' A man's voice boomed out.

'It's about the loco,' Cathy answered in a loud whisper.

'By Goy!' the man said. He slammed the window down.

The door creaked open. 'Come in, come in, hinny,' Mr. Stevens invited.

They went into a low-ceilinged living-room. The dog threatened them from a distant corner, like an approaching thunder-storm.

Mr. Stevens, who seemed to have slept in his corduroy trousers and pyjama jacket, levered a poker under the cinders in the fireplace and scattered some small branches on the top. In no time they were crouching on the thick clippy mat in front of a crackling fire.

'Wheesht now, Shap,' Mr. Stevens told the dog, at the same time looking at Cathy and Chas from under bushy white eyebrows. 'Now, lassie, what's all this about the loco?' Cathy drew a deep steadying breath and explained.

Mr. Stevens settled himself in a nest of cushions and knitted patchwork rugs, in an armchair, humming tunelessly all the time, nodding his head occasionally. He had a lot of white short hair, sticking up round his head. A thin moustache struggled to grow in the shade of his large hooked nose. Cathy thought that it looked as if he had used up too much hair on his head and eyebrows and hadn't left enough for a moustache as well. The firelight glowed on his face, which Cathy realised with a small shock, had skin a size too small so that it was stretched to cover the bones, just like her own Dad's, but quite unlike young Duggy's and Big Duggy's round features.

Mr. Stevens stared into the fire, flames reflecting and flaring in his bright blue eyes; humming away, until Cathy finished.

'And you think I should fire the loco now, to fetch them politicians up from Haltwhistle?' They nodded. 'Wey then, we'd better get a start, else it'll get over late.' He eased out of his nest.

'We knew you'd help,' Cathy's voice was emotional. 'I just knew!'

'Wey, we cannot let the likes o' yon villains win—they need takin' through hands.' Mr. Stevens shook his fist.

He unhooked some overalls from the back of the door and inserted his feet into the legs, then, bracing his knees outward to hold them up, he flung straps from the back, up over each shoulder, catching them at the front and fastening them, still humming away, watched by Cathy with open-mouthed admiration. Then he put on a donkey jacket and knotted a white silky knitted scarf round his pyjama jacket neck.

'Are ye comin' or not?' he said, pulling a pair of boots from under the table and stamping his feet into them. 'And don't forget the fire-guard, else we'll mebbe have the house afire.' He opened the door, hesitated, then went over to a press, the length and height of an entire wall. He opened a drawer and, stirring his hand round inside, found an old LNER cap. He pulled it on and adjusted the still shiny peak over his left ear and gave a final 'On guard, Shap,' to the excited dog.

'The keys!' Cathy exclaimed. 'Duggy said to remind you about the shed keys.'

Old Duggy patted his coat pocket. 'Aye, lassie, everything's in hand', he said as they left the house.

Reassured by the presence of a grown-up, they went down the back lane to the top of the steps.

'Just a minute,' Cathy said and dragged Chas up the short King's Arms Lane and round into the main street to inspect her mother's shop windows. They gazed at the treasures, arranged on rich russet velvet, which Cathy recognised as the curtains she had last seen hanging at the sitting-room windows, at Burnhaugh. In the centre of one window, the porcelain figures were displayed.

'Aren't they beautiful?' Cathy sighed. 'Mum hasn't half worked at this—I should've helped her, instead of being kidnapped . . . '

Chas had not paid much attention to Cathy; his nose was close to the door, the better to see a table full of model trains, china loco money-boxes, books, plates—all sorts of railway-orientated stock.

'Great!' he said. 'She should do well with this stuff—something for everybody!'

Old Duggy's head appeared round the corner and he demanded: 'Are you comin' or not?'

They caught up with Mr. Stevens in the lane and went down the steps, back to the station.

14

'Listen—I've been thinking,' Duggy announced. Tim and Simon groaned.

'Just when we thought it was safe to go out,' Tim said.

'We need help—we can't be everywhere. And just think, if there's more explosives buried and we don't find them and somebody gets blown up.' Duggy paused to draw breath, then went on: 'ALPS! The place is crammed with members—they'll be mad if anything goes wrong, after all the work they've put into the line. We could get a sort of posse together, spread out down the line, watch out for anybody suspicious....' He looked from one to the other. 'Well, what do you think?'

'Good idea,' Tim agreed. 'So long as the gang hasn't infiltrated ALPS—you never know.... '

'So long as they don't spoil our pitch—we don't want a lot of idiots running about the place, ruining everything,' Simon said.

'We won't tell them about taking the Daler to Halt-whistle—they'd all want to be on it,' Duggy said.

'Come on, we'll go and see what they say—they'll be in the café, likely, knocking back shandies. At least if we ask them, and they don't want to help, it'll be their fault if something goes wrong . . . '

Melly thought that it was no business of hers, so she held her peace, although she wondered at Duggy's logic. She was feeling the first twinge of boredom; she had not expected being left in a damp wood with three uncouth boys. They had taken little notice of her so far, so she felt justified in yawning loudly—for a well-brought-up girl—and wandering out of range of their utterly boring conversation about railways. After all, she hardly knew them, or Cathy, really. Cathy kept her company sometimes when her parents were away, but they had different tastes in most things. Now that Melly thought about the matter, she realised that she had nothing at all in common with these locals. Her mother didn't like her being too friendly with people like them. If she left now, she could just about catch the last bus—it was only a short walk at the other end, through the wood to the Lodge, and Tiny would come straight to the bus-stop, the moment she whistled. In spite of her mother's snobbish attitude towards Cathy and her friends, Melly couldn't help a stab of envy as she thought of their camaraderie and the fun they seemed to have; but, most of all, she envied them their sense of loyalty.

Melly had convinced herself that she had made a mistake in coming here—although it had seemed a good idea at the time and she admitted the railmotor trip had been great. But she had no desire to antagonise her parents by being absent from home if they phoned at the usual time.

'I've just remembered about a phone call—I'll catch a bus home, so don't worry, I'll be quite all right. 'Bye!' Melly said quickly, hurrying past the three boys.

She added brightly: 'And say goodbye to Cathy for me, won't you?'

The three watched open-mouthed as she ran off to catch the bus, which was parked outside the garage over the bridge on the opposite side of the valley.

'She'll be lucky,' Tim said. 'It's a goodish step, past the station and over to the garage.'

'Wonder why she left in such a rush—you'd think she would have stayed at home in the first place if she didn't want to come with Cathy,' Simon said. He was still under the impression that all girls were like Cathy: contradictory, gutsy and loyal, if given to odd outbursts. 'And what if her Dad's something to do with this gang—she might tell her folks about us, but mebbe not, if her parents told her not to mix with us rough boys.'

'Lasses!' Duggy snorted. 'Just a nuisance when they flounce off like that.'

'Well, Cathy's not back yet, is she?' Tim shrugged, 'And I suppose Melly will be OK going off on her own like that?'

Tim watched the bus, willing it not to leave until Melly was on it.

'She's used to looking after herself—independent and all that.' Simon assured him. 'It's not as if this is the jungle.' Then he thought of what had happened to them in the space of two days. 'Actually,' he added. 'I think she might be safer in the jungle....'

'Ah, there she is. She was a bit of a liability, really,' Tim said, 'She's caught the bus.... Now, where were we?'

'I was saying, we could divide the line into lengths—you know, so many ALPS members patrol from here to, say, Slaggyford, then the rest take the railmotor and do from Slaggyford to Lambley, and we can do the stretch from there to Haltwhistle in reverse.'

'We're going nearly as far as Haltwhistle with Grandad and the Daler. We'll have time to nip back to Lambley and check, although we know the viaduct's OK now. We can ask the ALPS folk to start after we have got well away from Alston, else they'll be livid if they see us on the loco when they're trudging down the line. They can have a bit nap before they go—and we and the Daler'll be out of the way of the railmotor.'

'You know what I think?' Simon said. 'I think we should eat

some of those jam sandwiches we made this morning—I'm starving! It's ages since we had anything, which is funny when you think, 'cos usually all Duggy thinks about is food.'

'Boredom—that's what makes people overeat. That, and hunger.'

'Well, if you don't want your sandwiches, Tim, I'll tidy them up for you,' Duggy grinned. 'Then we'll nip into the café and buy some juice or something, later—when we round ALPS up.'

Old Duggy heaved himself up on to the footplate.

Chas, Tim, Simon and Cathy watched admiringly as old Duggy tried the dampers, checked water levels and smokebox, ran a greasy rag round the firebox door edge, made sure the ashpan was cleared, noted deflector and protector plates were in position. Then he made up the fire.

'I thought all you had to do was chuck a few sticks on and a bucket of coal and go away till the boiler heated. I didn't realise there was so much to do,' Tim said, but Mr. Stevens merely hummed— a deeply contented hum.

The Daler glowed; her new LNER livery shone; her brass-work was almost blindingly burnished. A full bunker of best coal glinted; water tanks were filled to capacity; the 0–6–0 was ready and waiting.

'There's something about engines, isn't there?' Cathy said, glancing round the cab. 'Specially steam—all that power.' Her initial hurt over Melly's desertion had faded to a feeling of: 'Well, if that's how she feels, just wait till she asks me to keep her company again.'

Old Duggy tended his fire carefully, almost stroking coal in at each side, then over the front edge below the firedoor. When this cleared, he put on another couple of shovelfuls at one side, then, when it brightened, a couple more at the other side.

He adjusted the dampers and firedoor to get the right amount of air to the fire. Once the water level and the pressure started to rise and the blower was turned on, he stopped humming and turned to face his audience. His moustache had found enough strength to bristle. He was not a smiler, but his brows lifted slightly and his eyes were bright. He was evidently pleased with the way things were going. 'She's goin' nicely,' he said. 'Little an' often, that's the way to feed a loco—just like a bairn.' He tipped his cap further on to one side and fished a pipe out of his pyjama pocket, lit it, and drew in a great gasp of smoke.

'What a performance,' Cathy thought. 'ALPS should sell tickets and charge people for watching if there's this kind of show every time'

'Grandad,' Duggy said, 'you'll know about the geli we found on Lambley viaduct?'

'Aye!' Big Duggy's teeth snapped shut on his pipe stem. 'Blasted varmints!' He shovelled more coal, filled in a hole or two and shut the firebox door. He waved his shovel about.

'Aa'll brain them with this if Aa lay hands on them. If Aa can find any brains . . . '

Encouraged by regular fuelling, the boiler pressure rose gradually.

The old man began to reminisce, while the young folk listened, spellbound, to his tales of the days of earlier steam on the Alston Line.

He told them of rivalry between drivers, and the time when one engine was tampered with at Haltwhistle, pulled into Slaggyford station with water dangerously low, and all the passengers formed a chain and passed the ladies' bonnets full of water from the well to the loco, until the level was high enough to get them to Alston and the water tank. Cathy was charmed by this; she could imagine the scene—all those soggy bonnets.

'Mind, there was ructions when the top brass got to know. The driver was sacked, and the fireman was hauled ower the coals.' They all groaned at old Duggy's pun.

He told them of the war years when the royal train was parked overnight in Featherstone cutting, and of the bombs that were dropped near Burnstones viaduct.

He told them about the great snowstorm in 1947, when the line was blocked and some of the German prisoners of war helped to dig it out.

Then there was the poaching that went on, although old Duggy had no personal experience, he said....

Old Duggy checked the pressure: 'Hundred and forty.' He nodded at Duggy.

'Is that it?' Duggy asked. He looked so excited that Cathy thought that *he* would blow off steam.

'Aye. We'll couple up the coaches, then we'll be away. It's gettin' on for twelve, an' we don't want to be rushing about—we'll just go canny. Mind, I don't see how we can get to Plainmellor without somebody noticin'. But it'll likely not matter.' He tamped his pipe out on the handrail and looked at Duggy from under his bushy eyebrows: 'Now laddie, I need a fireman—and seein' as you're the only one dressed for work, mebbe you'll stand in?'

Duggy's face grew even more flushed and excited. He grabbed the shovel. The loco edged out of the shed, pistons moving deliberately, smoothly.

Tim and Chas jumped down to close the shed doors when the engine was clear. After signalling their intention with much waving of arms, they went off in the direction of the café, to find as many ALPS members as were available.

Duggy changed the points and the Daler continued on to the main line and steamed up to the platform. Duggy almost fell off the footplate in his haste to connect the coaches. The engine gently edged up, touched buffers, parted and touched again. There was a satisfying chunky sound as iron met iron. Duggy leapt back on to the loco and they slid away from the platform to wait for Chas and Tim.

The gas lamps on the platform were out, but yellow oblongs of light showed the twins where to find their men; waiting-room, café and shop were all inhabited. Somebody was vacuuming, by the sound of it, Tim thought with a grin: of all the times! He thumbed down the sneck and opened the café door.

Tim did a swift head count—twenty. Nobody took any notice; they were all serious-looking, crouched four to a table.

They went on talking, gesticulating, arguing. Olive vacuumed in corners, preparing for tomorrow. Whatever else was going on, Olive's café would be clean for the big day. Chas nudged Tim's elbow and they stumbled down the steps, still half-blinded by the sudden light.

Olive saw them and switched off the vacuum. The ALPS members sat silent and watchful. Then they heard the sound which was as dear to them as their life's blood: the Daler connecting with the coaches. Light dawned on twenty faces, then was extinguished as they realised that somebody was making off with their loco.

Chairs were pushed back; boots clattered on the floor.

Tim pulled himself together and started a speech.

'I can explain,' he began, then Olive came over and put an arm round his shoulder.

'You know who these two are?' she asked the members. 'Two of the kidnapped youngsters. Come on lads—explain.'

Tim and Chas took turns in telling their story, as far as they thought necessary, stalling for time, to allow old Duggy to be in position for a quick getaway.

They omitted their theory on the assassination of the VIPs.

'So we thought it would be a good idea if you went and

checked for explosives—in case they've planted some more,' Tim finished, pleased at the effect his tale was having.

'You mean you've come from Lambley in that clapped-out railmotor, not knowing if you were going to be blown up?' one of them asked, looking from Tim to Chas as if he couldn't believe his ears.

'Well, we were pretty sure we wouldn't be—not tonight, anyway. They wouldn't have any reason for doing anything tonight—it would be wasted. But tomorrow, now, they might let rip.'

'They might try to blow both engines up, if they don't get hold of the plans.' This explanation sounded thin to Tim, but the members understood the reasoning behind it, as Duggy had. What could be more important than the plans of a new loco?

'The railmotor is on the sidings—but you'll need to fill her up in case the carb blocks again, so if you can find some petrol....' Two men strode out, muttering something about 'carboots', 'torches', 'spares'.

'And your party'll search from Lambley to Haltwhistle?' somebody asked.

The twins nodded. 'As long as you wait till we get well in front with the Daler—we don't want the railmotor too close in behind us. I thought mebbe if there's a can of tea—a sandwich or two.... It's just that we haven't had a proper meal since—' He had to think: 'It was early breakfast, I think....' Tim was a master of the pathetic.

Olive was in the kitchen before he had finished.

Kettles were filled.

The café emptied as the members went to inspect the loco; Tim and Chas made for the kitchen.

Duggy's mother was toasting oatmeal in a cast-iron pan and liquidising soup, in between shaking the oats. Covered bowls of raspberries were defrosting on a bench.

Tomorrow's guests were going to do pretty well. Tim and Chas recognised the signs. There would be whipped cream to mix with the fruit and oats.

Duggy's mother turned to squeezing lemons for a sorbet, pausing only to nod. Tim remembered that Duggy had told his mother that they were safe—or at least, Duggy had been safe at the time, which would explain her evident absence of worry.

His own parents would never understand what was happening, even if they heard what had been going on at Slaggyford. Mrs. Stevens, a cool customer, had evidently not told Olive that she knew everybody was safe. Olive's surprise had been genuine enough.

A large fish-kettle sat on the stove. Somebody had mentioned South Tyne salmon and Alston Moor lamb....

Olive poured tea and milk into old-fashioned tea-cans, and stirred sugar with a generous hand.

'Duggy's Grandad'll recognise these,' she said, clamping the lids on tightly. 'They're like the ones he used when he was a full-time driver.' She handed each of them a large plastic box. 'Sorry, lads—it's only sandwiches again, but we're up to the eyes, getting ready for tomorrow. You can't get on when folks are sitting about, getting under your feet.'

Cathy peeped round the kitchen door, having been overcome with shyness at the sight of the ALPS members in the café.

'Hello,' she said brightly, when Mrs. Stevens smiled at her without speaking. They all knew Mrs. Stevens. When she was into her stride nothing would deflect her. She would be repeating in her head what else was to do for tomorrow. Cathy was glad that she had escaped to the kitchen. She sucked a frozen raspberry and surveyed the preparations.

'Anything I can help with?' she asked. Mrs. Stevens turned a stony face on her.

'Certainly not!' she snapped. 'Just look at you—you're as bad as our Duggy!' Then she smiled and gave them each a glass of unfrozen sorbet. 'But you can come and help with the dishes tomorrow,' she added.

'Time to go; they'll be wanting to get on.' Tim said hastily; he handed back his empty glass and backed away. 'Thanks very much, both.'

'And mind—don't get into any more mischief,' Mrs.Stevens called after them.

Cathy paused outside the door to sniff a trough full of wallflowers.

'Mmm, lovely! My favourite flowers, I think....'

'Come on you, and never mind the gardening,' Tim said, steering her through the throng round the loco.

Envious eyes watched as the teenagers climbed back on to the footplate. There was a chorus of 'See you later', 'Enjoy yourselves', and a few 'Be carefuls'. Then, with much waving and whistling, the members made for the railmotor.

Simon volunteered to open the trap points at Slaggyford and Lambley. Mr. Stevens nodded and adjusted the levers; Duggy opened the firebox door so that to the people watching from the sidings they seemed to be disappearing in a traditional blaze of glory.

Smooth and powerful, the Daler's rods and pistons increased their speed as old Duggy opened the regulator. He jammed his cap more firmly over his ear, hunched his shoulders and glowered. There was a wild light at the back of his eyes.

The loco pounded down the line. Some people heard the remembered sounds on the night air, and smiled.

Cathy and Simon, Tim and Chas, became steam enthusiasts that night; for how could they help it when its very power vibrated under their feet? They imbibed the taste, the feel, the smell, of steam, and were intoxicated by it. The air was filled with the magic of it.

Duggy had already imbibed, with his mother's milk.

Pistons, cylinders, wheels—the entire loco throbbed with controlled energy as the heavy engine raced northwards, hauling its wake of carriages.

There was a wild light at the back of Duggy's eyes, too, as he flung coal into the firebox like a mad thing, until old Duggy restrained him.

'She'll start to blow off at yon end if you put overmuch in—it'll make an awful row at this late hour.'

It ended, too soon.

'Check points,' Old Duggy said for the last time. Four volunteers jumped down to oblige him and, as before, found the points set for the sidings.

Old Duggy slipped his engine into Plenmellor sidings, just short of the sand drag, and damped the fire down, temporarily, until it would be required to haul the train into Haltwhistle, in time for the big-wigs' journey back to Alston.

Cathy's eyes were brilliant.

'That was just—marvellous. I wouldn't have missed it for anything. I say, can you get women loco-drivers?'

Everybody laughed then, and relaxed, as if they had reached the end of a race—having won it.

'Better have our bait now, then a bit rest afore daylight,' Old Duggy reached for his tea-can. Cathy opened the sandwich-boxes and handed them round in the light of the waning moon.

She nibbled the crusts first, keeping the egg and cressy middle bit till last. Simon ate the middle first; for him, the crust was the best part. Tim and Chas started at one corner and ate steadily, taking almost identical bites.

'Those ALPS members'll be tired in the morning,' Tim mumbled through a mouthful of sticky gingerbread. He wiped crumbs from his mouth. 'They'll be up all night, dodging about on the line.'

Cathy rolled her eyes. 'Mmm—Duggy, your mother is the best cook in the north.'

Duggy grinned happily.

'Don't tell our Mum,' Simon murmured.

They left old Duggy watchful on his simmering hotplate, as Cathy insisted on calling it, and climbed into a coach to try and rest until daylight.

'Here—' Simon grabbed Cathy as she was about to sit on one of the luxuriously upholstered seats. 'We can't sit on these posh seats—not the state we're in. I mean, just look at us. And the VIPs will be coming in here, with their designer ensembles. We'll just have to sit on the floor.'

'Well, it's got carpet on it. Anyway, if we've saved their lives, they're not going to worry over a bit of dust, are they?'

'She's right,' Tim agreed. 'Only it's not dust we're covered in—it's moss and peat and leaf-mould and I dunno what-all!'

'Cath—remember that chocolate you pinched out of my pocket the other day?'

'Oh, yes. So I did. I'd forgotten all about that, Duggy. Why? D'ye want it back?' Cathy delved into her jeans pocket.

'No! It's been sat on, melted, set, kidnapped, smoked on the footplate....No thanks, but you can have it if you like..'

'I would leave well alone, if I were you,' Tim advised. 'From where I was looking earlier it didn't look very healthy. I wish you'd said—it might have saved our lives back at Lambley.'

'Well, what now?' Cathy asked, glancing out at the ghostly silver birches and willows on the overgrown colliery site. 'What can we do now? It's practically the middle of the night. We're almost nocturnal.'

'Not a lot,' Duggy admitted, 'except keep a look-out. We're supposed to be resting, but I never felt less like sleeping than I do now.'

'Our brains are over-active,' Chas said in his solemn voice.

'Oh—come on—let's wander up to Lambley now, and check for anything out of the ordinary.' Simon opened the carriage door and jumped down.

'Have you any ideas on whereabouts the gang might be?' Duggy asked, following him out.

Simon shrugged. 'Be like looking for a tadpole in a prog fond. We'll recognise the ones we've seen—or heard—but there'll be more than that in the gang, wouldn't you say?'

'That's just Ginger and the others from the Range Rover, and Chuck's voice—I'll never forget that!' Chas said. 'American or Canadian, he was. We'll never forget any of them.'

'This is the hardest part—the waiting,' Tim said morosely. He brightened. 'Why don't we mooch about, like we used to do years ago—remember? There used to be a badger's sett somewhere along the river—past the prisoner-of-war camp at Featherstone, wasn't it?'

'Well, there's nothing of that left now—the camp, I mean. But we're going that way to Lambley anyway—not that there'll be much to see.' Simon sighed reminiscently. 'We spent hours watching the badgers—and Mum never knew that we'd been out all night. At least,' Simon added, 'not until she found our shoes.'

'You just said "prog fond",' Cathy giggled. 'Like you used to when you were young.'

Simon jogged her arm with his elbow to shut her up. Chas continued as if he had not been interrupted by badgers.

'But don't forget we've got two of the gang—we haven't got them to worry about. It's the other ones—the ones we haven't got— that we're looking for.'

'Oh, they'll show up in the morning,' Simon said.

'Nine for ten . . . If our theory's correct,' Chas amended.

They glanced back at old Duggy's pipe glowing from the cab, then merged into the lineside undergrowth.

'It's like stealing time, isn't it? Being out at night, I mean, when we're not supposed to be. As if we've got a few extra hours from somewhere, when most folks are wasting their time sleeping,' Cathy whispered.

'We seem to be making a heck of a row. We'll frighten all the wildlife for miles around—not to mention the gang,' Simon murmured, dodging a low branch.

'I wonder what the police are doing? They'll have to be here tomorrow to look after the VIPs—they normally do. Only they won't know about the threat from Chuck's lot, they'll still think it's the plans the gang's after,' Chas said. 'And it's May Day. They couldn't have picked a better day for an assassination—everything happens on May Day—political rallies, football matches, charity runs, the lot! The police'll be stretched pretty thin, I'd say.'

'Just fancy, if you hadn't found that geli on the viaduct, we could all've been blown up!' Cathy gasped, as if she had just realised.

'We never discovered who was—or is—going to push the button. As far as the gang knows, that geli is still wired up. It must be somebody local, or else somebody's coming back to finish the job.' Simon was thinking aloud. 'Just as well ALPS are hanging about up there.'

'There's no sign of them, yet. Must be pretty quiet.' Tim said.

They had reached the north end of the viaduct. They climbed over on to the line and began their search for signs of—well, they weren't sure....

'We'd better be quiet now—and spread out. Keep your head down, Cathy,' Simon warned. 'Although they could have taken a pot at us any time, I suppose, if they'd wanted to—or if they'd been here.'

'Sitting ducks.' Chas nodded. 'That's what we are. I'm pretty certain that the gang won't show up until "nine for ten" in the morning.'

'They seem to come and go as they like—terrorists, I mean,' Duggy muttered, searching the line for signs of disturbance. 'Who was it again? Les somebody or other—was supposed to have claimed they blew up that airliner at Christmas over Alaska—a Jumbo jet, with one of the Yankee high-ups on board. Then it was Rome last Easter—another plane blown up. An embassy in Paris in the backend....'

'And Haltwhistle on May Day?' Simon finished.

'I'll never forget those men at Alston,' Cathy shivered. 'The way they looked at us, when Duggy told them what he thought of them....'

They stared at each other, remembering, their faces blanched by moonlight.

'It's a wonder they didn't knock us off on the spot,' Simon said, cold, sheer horror rising sickly in his stomach as he recalled the expressions on the faces of the three men.

Instinctively Tim put his hand in his pocket and gripped the cold metal of Chuck's revolver. Chas, watching, said nothing, but he looked grim, and turned away to look down the track. At last Tim spoke: 'Well, if you're going to be kidnapped, I suppose you feel better if it's done by professionals—and this lot certainly aren't amateurs..'

'It was only a fluke they missed capturing Duggy,' Simon said

'And Ginger's the only one that knows that!' Duggy added, rubbing his head. 'And he'll not tell!'

'He's out of action—unless somebody's found him in the Land Rover. But it doesn't matter, now.'

'Hey—you don't suppose we could be had up, for kidnapping Ginger—and Chuck, do you?' Simon gulped at the thought.

'No—it'll all blow over, likely,' Tim said.

Chas looked at him sharply. 'Or Up . . . '

Searching thoroughly their stretch of line, they worked their way back to Plenmellor.

Their train was in sight, but they did not feel inclined to sit on the corridor carpet again, so instead they sat on a fallen tree.

'Well, what are we going to do?' Tim asked impatiently. 'We can't sit about here talking, while that lot set about killing half the Government. We'll have to stick together—be safer that way.'

'No!' Chas contradicted. 'We'll separate. They might spot one of us, but the rest will still be left—they can't find all of us, not if we're scattered. And separated, we've got more chances of finding the gang.'

'Cathy comes with me,' Tim said flatly. 'After all, I've got the gun.'

'Why don't we all pool our ideas, instead of squabbling? Like—how do we cross the Tyne? I mean, we can't all just troop down the railway and over the Alston Arches viaduct. If it was up to me, I would say Cath and Tim should cross on the old road bridge—it's closed to traffic, but you can still walk between the bollards.' Duggy put his hands into his boiler-suit pockets.

'One of us could go by the Alston Arches—me. I mean, I

look more like a railwayman than any of you lot—boiler suit and that. The station staff'll be on the lookout for trespassers on the lines—photographers'll do anything to get an unusual shot—but they might not notice me. I'll keep well down, behind the viaduct parapet wall. Once I'm across, I can keep a lookout from the Alston side of the platform, OK?'

'So that leaves Chas and me,' Simon said, tapping his front teeth with a thumb-nail, considering the alternative routes into Haltwhistle. 'We could leave the line above Bellister Castle and walk down the road alongside the Tyne, cross on the new bridge and come in at the west end on the A69. That way we'll cover all the town, between us.'

'Right! And we'll hunt in pairs—except for Duggy. Cathy and I'll walk down the line to the Plenmellor bridge, shin down the embankment on to the road, cross the old road bridge and under the Newcastle-Carlisle line overbridge, on to the A69 and turn east to the town foot, then work back through the town to the station. OK, Duggy?'

Duggy nodded. 'We'll have to concentrate on the station, mind. That's where the action's going to be. The VIPs aren't going into Haltwhistle at all—they'll hop off the main-line train and cross over the footbridge and into our train. I mean, Alston's where the meal and the reception and everything'll be. A town saved by the railway, one of the papers called it.'

'It'll do a bit of good for Haltwhistle as well—all those rail enthusiasts and visitors spending money. Funny, isn't it, calling a town Haltwhistle? It would be built round the railway, I expect,' Tim said, hoping Duggy wouldn't launch into a complete history of the Industrial Revolution.

Still, the railway probably would save Alston from extinction, and from being cut off in the winter with no means of transport. With Unicus parts to manufacture, there would be work for a foundry and other light industries, employing townsfolk.

'Now this is interesting!' Simon stood up and stretched cramped legs. 'Haltwhistle is a corruption of the old name, pronounced something like Hod-i-sill, Celtic possibly—nothing to do with railways. It's an ancient town—"castle on a hill at the meeting of the waters", it means. The moat hill has modern houses built on it, but it's still called Castle Hill. Tell you what, some day in the holidays we'll come down and have a good hunt round'

'Right.' Tim sounded less than enthusiastic, but then,he was a one job at a time man. 'If we're out of jail by then.'

'Talking about jail, what about your Grandad, Dug? I mean, he's getting on a bit and there's bound to be an inquest when all this is over. We've as good as pinched the loco, us and your Grandad.'

'Come on, Si. Grandad knows a lot more than he lets on. He was going to drive the loco in any case—he's just done it a bit earlier, that's all. Mind you, his rostered fireman wouldn't be very chuffed at four o'clock this morning when he turned up and found the loco and Grandad gone. He'll be OK though.'

They laughed uneasily.

Cathy's face whitened as she listened to the others. She clenched her hands in her pockets.

'I'll count to ten and wake up at home,' she thought desperately. 'People like us don't go about looking for murderers—terrorists—or being kidnapped by them, or travelling over viaducts filled with explosives, on steam locos with bushy-browed drivers in pyjama jackets and mufflers. I'll wake up soon; I know I will.'

She felt her finger-nails, like so many pins, sticking into her palms and tried to relax.

Glancing round at the four boys, she recognised the tension in them too: the sharp expression in their eyes; the widening of the pupils; the tightening of mouth and chin muscles; and, most significant, the irrelevant chat. Even if they're as scared as I am, they've got to go on. They—we—are too far in now to back out.

'Besides,I owe them one for this!' Simon was saying. He patted the bump on his head.

'We all owe them one—' Tim stood up. 'I'd like to land one on the cretin who planned all this.'

'Well, I'll go and tell Grandad what we're doing. It's about half past six anyway—time to go. We'll have about three hours to search for the gang.'

Duggy paused uncertainly, aware that he was required to say something but too embarrassed to say what was in his mind. He polished his dishevelled hair as if to massage a brilliant parting message out of his brain, but in the end he mumbled 'See you' and cantered off into the grey dawn-light.

'We'd better be off as well. We've got further to walk than you two, so we'll push off now.' Simon zipped up his anorak with unnecessary force.

Cathy licked her dry lips and forced them to form the words: 'Take care,' she croaked.

'You too,' Simon and Chas replied quietly, waved, and were gone.

Duggy hoisted himself on to the footplate, surprising his Grandad, who was staring down the line, cold pipe in hand, remembering journeys past and crews long gone.

Quickly Duggy explained their plan.

'Right, lad, we'll get the better of them beggars yet.' He knocked his pipe out and refilled it. Duggy watched the untidy shreds of tobacco ignite as old Duggy sucked and blew, making small plopping sounds. Looking at his grandson over the top of his pipe, he said: 'I'd better tell you now—the new loco and your father are down yonder.' He flicked a spent match Haltwhistlewards. He added with dry understatement: 'We reckoned somebody'd be interested in the loco . . . so we stabled it down this end.'

Duggy felt the layers of fear he had carried about peel off, as he realised that his Dad really was safe. In spite of the cryptic telephone message, he had wondered.

The two Stevenses exchanged a long understanding look—then Duggy was off, jogging down the line.

Mr. Stevens sighed and shook his head as he watched Duggy's chunky figure out of sight. Where would this business end, he wondered. As queer a do as ever he could remember—and he could remember a few. He chuckled, thinking of old Bas, his fireman, turning up at four o'clock to fire the Daler and finding the shed empty. Still, Duggy's mother would explain. It wouldn't stop old Bas from being narked, though. Better get a bit more steam up ready for the off.

15

In a bedroom at the Railway Hotel, a middle-aged hiker—*the
middle-aged hiker*—switched on the bedside light, depressed
the alarm-clock button, reached for his spectacles and sat on
the edge of the bed, instantly wide awake. First scratching his
dark hair vigorously, he pulled on a fawnish, greyish wig, like
a woollen tea-cosy. He then removed the chair with which he
had wedged the door shut last night, checked that his
rucksack was where he had left it, and hopped back into bed
as footsteps approached and stopped outside his door.

'Mr. Robinson?' a tentative voice enquired.

'Come in, come in, Mrs. Waite,' the hiker called, his eyes
watchful as Mrs.Waite came in, carrying a breakfast tray. His
hand, covering a revolver underneath the quilt, relaxed a
little. 'You are very punctual.'

'Good morning, Mr Robinson. Although, mind you, it is
misty, but the forecast's good, so let's hope everything goes off
well.'

'I hope so too, Mrs. Waite,' Mr. Robinson murmured
fervently.

Mrs. Waite bustled about, setting his breakfast on a
bed-table and sliding it into position over Mr. Robinson's
knees, chatting in her lilting Northumbrian accent.
'Everything all right for you? You'll need a good meal inside
you if you're going off walking all day. There! And if you need
anything else you've only to ring the bell.'

What he really wanted to say was: 'Shut up and get out, woman.' But he was for the time being a bumbling, middle-aged hiker and railway enthusiast.

'Thank you Mrs. Waite—very nice I'm sure,' he said mildly, picking up his grapefruit spoon and watching Mrs. Waite over the top of his glasses until she closed the door.

He ate quickly and efficiently, emptied the coffee-pot and, leaning back on the pillows, considered the hours ahead.

Unconsciously he reached out to replace the coffee-pot cosy and realign his knife and fork. A fanatically tidy soul, Mr. Robinson.

Better start with a leisurely amble along the street to collect a newspaper, then back for his coffee at nine-thirty, collect his packed lunch—then, as far as Mrs. Waite knew, that was him out for the day, walking along the Roman wall.

'I don't care for the madding crowd you know, Mrs. Waite,' he would tell her confidentially. 'I shall come back later to travel on the Alston line when the first fine careless rapture has worn off. Meanwhile I shall call on my friend in the signal-box, take a photograph or two, then I'm off for the day—over the hills and far away.' This was always the most difficult part of the operation; he must act the part until the last second, disarm any suspicion before it took root.

Having showered, dressed, and combed his wig, he patted his gun-pocket, checked that his belongings were packed into his bulky rucksack, then opened the heavy velvet curtains. He looked out at the day. To right and left traffic roared past on the main road, with occasional deviation when a vehicle turned off the road to enter the town. He heard them changing gear at the junction, behind the hotel, out of his sight. Already people were hurrying towards the station, staking their claims to a view of the opening ceremony.

Suddenly he was convulsed with silent laughter. Opening ceremony—that was a good one....

Recovering his composure, he gave a last assessing look over the road towards the station. The signal-box lights glowed through the slight mist which lay like a bloom on the river valley. He saw the signalman moving about, the row of levers silhouetted like miniature tank-traps against the light.

People crossed from the north-side platform, over the cast-iron footbridge to the Alston platform and waiting-room, which lay like an island between the main Newcastle-Carlisle line and the Alston line and sidings.

From the window he could just see heads and shoulders of people on the bridge—but this was all he needed to see. He had chosen this window, that bridge, weeks ago, on an earlier visit.

Just beyond and below the signalbox there would be parked a black police van, first of a chain of escape vehicles. Nothing was left to chance.

Satisfied, he went to the door, adopting as he went the slightly stooped, hunched shoulders, the slow steps, of an older man.

Only one thing remained. He intercepted a now harassed Mrs .Waite, who decided at that moment that there must be easier ways of earning a living.

'Oh, there you are. Did I mention that I'm expecting my daughter to call on me today? She might be here quite soon—Robina, my daughter.' He leaned forward confidentially and lowered his voice. 'She's a journalist, you know—London paper—has to do an article on the Alston line reopening. Take some pictures—local colour, you know.'

Mrs Waite nodded. Silly old fool, she thought, wearing what looked like a tabby cat on his head.

She wished he would let go of her arm or she would never get finished in time, and she thought: 'I'll bet he's left his pyjamas on the side of the bath again—they'll be to dry . . . ' Blue and white striped flannelette pyjamas and a quite expensive dressing-gown were awaiting her attention; Mr. Robinson had left them to allay any suspicion that he intended not to return to pay his not inconsiderable bill. He continued:

'I suggested she use my little eyrie—so convenient. She has a portable typewriter—telescopic lens camera. The view from my room is more than adequate. You will see that she is not disturbed—lot of pressure involved—ambitious. I knew you wouldn't mind. Now I'm going for my little constitutional—collect my yellow rag. I don't care much for crowds, you know, Mrs. Waite—' And he trotted out his little speech before wandering out to the newsagents and back in time for a quick coffee.

Mr.Robinson sipped his excellent coffee and scanned his newspaper, then collected his rucksack and quite calmly, sauntered out of the hotel and made his way to the signal-box. He climbed up the steps, waving to Tot as he approached the door. The police van was in position between the river and the railway, midway between the signal-box and an access tunnel under the branch line.

He noticed that the steam loco had already arrived at the platform and was surrounded by a crowd—it would keep them out of his way.

A quarter of a mile away, the viaduct, known locally as the Alston Arches, carried the Alston branch line southward in a wide sweeping curve over the Tyne and up into the Northern Pennines. The high embankment on the far side of the river was a patchwork of yellow broom and white hawthorn blossoms and fresh green leaves.

Mr. Robinson was not so much interested in the local flora; he was more interested in the television company's van parked near the northern abutment of the Alston arches. He watched keenly as the crew ran about with cameras, lights—and wires

'Morning, Tot,' he beamed affably. 'Sun going to get out for our big day, is it?'

'Mr. Robinson—you're not supposed to be here—you're trespassing, you know. I mean, it's all right you coming when there's not much doing, but the train from Carlisle will be in, any minute—all the big nobs—' Tot waved at the indicator panel in front of him; a green light showed on the diagram. 'See—it's in this section now!' Tot advanced on Mr. Robinson. 'Do me a favour and push off—you'll lose me my job, standing about chatting—'

'Tot!' Mr. Robinson snapped. 'Shut up and get on with your work—I'm here to see that you aren't interrupted—under-cover—security.' And he waved his revolver under Tot's nose, knowing that only he and Tot could see the gun.

'What? Oh, well—right!' Tot gaped at the formerly genial Mr. Robinson and his threatening gun. Rotten old so-and-so sneaking about, and all the time he's some sort of inspector. He put his mind back to the job in hand. The train was past the Spital distant signal; the train full of V.I.P.s would be easing in, any minute now.

Mr. Robinson leaned against the door-frame and gazed across to the Railway Hotel. As he watched, somebody slid open the lower sash of his bedroom window. Something small and round, like a lens, glinted on the sill, then steadied as the person inside settled it more firmly on the tripod resting on Mrs. Waite's floral Wilton.

Mr. Robinson fumbled in his pocket and pulled out a large white handkerchief. He held it folded in his palm, ready to unfurl and wave it at the crucial moment at his unseen daughter in the window opposite,.

The special train reached the end of the long cutting. As it came under the road bridge and into the station, the passengers collected raincoats, briefcases and handbags, straightened ties and hats, flicked imaginary dust from sleeves.

Mr. Robinson heard the rumble of the approaching train, saw the flurry of local councillors and ALPS officials as they assembled on the crowded platform below to greet the VIPs.

His handkerchief would be the signal to tell his 'daughter' in the bedroom window that the first of the VIPs had stepped on to the bottom steps of the footbridge and was about to cross.

The marksman would do the rest. She would see each of the targets in her sights long enough to pot them, one by one, like clay pigeons as they crossed the bridge. It would be over in seconds.

With the last pigeon down, a second wave of his handkerchief would warn the TV crew that it was time to start on the Alston Arches 'diversion'. Lestrange had said in their last tape-recorded briefing. 'Divert the attention of the police and the crowds by blasting the railway bridges—a few seconds after the shooting. Use your excellent judgement. But be accurate. Too early an explosion and our targets will dive for cover. Self-preservation is the most fundamental human

instinct. The railway bridges must not be blown up until the
last target is downed! Is that quite clear? Under cover of the
confusion you will—all of you—escape and make your way to
Port Ryan, as arranged. You know what to do. Good luck!'

Mr. Robinson felt his muscles tighten. Beads of perspiration
collected on his upper lip under the theatrical old-man's
make-up. He dared not wipe them away in case the
marksman misconstrued the movement. He was aware that
the marksman's long-distance lenses were focused on the
signal-box—on himself—most of the time.

Deliberately he forced himself to relax—toes, knees,
stomach, shoulders and neck muscles. The tension built up
again immediately. The thought passed through his mind that
he was sick of earning his living this way. Chasing on its heels,
the thought of Lestrange's revenge should the job be bungled.

From the corner of his eye he saw Tot moving about in the
signal-box. Poor unsuspecting Tot, he thought; playing with
his train sets.

'Undercover security man, indeed!'

Mr. Robinson felt another fit of silent laughter brewing—
they were becoming more frequent lately. He held in his
stomach muscles until the fit faded

By five minutes to ten Lestrange's men were in position.

By five minutes to ten the challenging team were in
position, although only five of them knew it.

Robina Robinson greeted Mrs. Waite and was shown her
father's room. She took her time, walking up the stairs;
relishing the feel of her long blonde hair swinging round her
silk-shirted shoulders; the feel of her fashionable suede skirt
swinging in unison with her hair. The heavy shoulder-bag,
presumably, held her camera and typewriter.

Mrs. Waite watched her enviously. Fancy old Robinson

having such a glamorous, expensive-looking daughter; you just never knew....

Once in the bedroom, Robina swung her heavy bag to the floor, wedged a chair under the doorknob, and crossed to the window. She stared out.

Max—Mr. Robinson—was good. He had chosen the perfect position from which to take out their targets. Lestrange's victims were always known as 'targets'.

Quickly she unzipped the bag and removed cotton-wrapped parcels. Methodically she assembled them: the parts of an extremely sophisticated automatic weapon. She fixed it on the tripod, adjusted the sights.

Her blue eyes darkened as she zoomed in on Max. He made an excellent middle-aged hiker, she thought, amused. One movement of her right hand and she could take him out. He was becoming quite odd. At one time she had been fond of him, but as far as Max and the rest of Lestrange's gang were concerned, she was herself a man. *Le gentil homme,* she thought. A man, like Max, with the ability to disguise himself as a woman when occasion demanded. Little did they know that Robina, high-powered journalist, and Alice middle-aged eccentric, or Ricky, driver of fast cars, or Lionel, middle- of-the-road politician, were some of her many disguises.

One or two longer-serving members of Lestrange's gang had seen her in perhaps a couple of different 'characters' but none of them had any idea of the vast range of disguises she could assume. In fact, she thought, sometimes she herself had difficulty in remembering who she—or he—really was....

Nine fifty five. Coolly, she lit a cigarette and checked the footbridge in her sights, then concentrated on Mr. Robinson, watching for the fatherly wave of the white handkerchief. After that it was up to her. She imagined the heads of her targets moving over the footbridge.

Imagined them lined up against the iron parapet, like sitting ducks in one of those fairground shooting games.

The train would be on time today....

She remembered the impressive value of the cheque which would soon be winging its way to Switzerland. She smiled.

She ground out her cigarette in Mrs. Waite's treasured Maling lustre fruit-bowl.

A few yards away, its tyres not quite nudging the kerb outside the Railway Hotel entrance, a black Jaguar waited. Jack, Robina's driver, sat behind the wheel.

He checked the time.

Two minutes to go.

He switched on the ignition and watched the hotel doorway....

Suddenly a uniformed policeman appeared in his nearside wing mirror. He inspected the car, as policemen do.

Jack sat quite relaxed, secure in the knowledge that everything was in order; documents OK. Twenty minutes parking limit, and he had only been parked for ten. Far enough from the junction not to be a hazard.

Timing was the essence of Lestrange's success. Jack would neither hear nor see Robina's gun firing, but he could depend on her exact timing, and she on his.

One would, he thought, be hard put to hear the Last Trump above the racket at the station. The Silver Band had started up now.

He did, however, expect to hear and see the explosion on the railway bridge. That would get rid of this officious copper.

He checked his watch again. Twenty seconds.

The policeman rapped on the side window and leaned down to peer in.

Still calm, Jack opened the window, and looked up enquiringly: 'Yes, officer?'

'I recognised your car, sir....'

Jack's heartbeat accelerated but he forced himself to appear nonchalant.

'Oh, yes?'

'The driver—it wasn't yourself, of course, sir, but he came into the police station at Hexham. Reported a missing Range Rover. Well, the Rover was found at Alston on Saturday. I thought you might like to know—perhaps get in touch with your friend or whoever owns it. We haven't contacted him yet, but if you could tell him it's found, well, it might put his mind at rest.'

Deny everything, Jack thought, then realised that this busybody was only being friendly and informative.

'Ah! Yes! My friend will certainly be pleased—my word, yes! Thank you very much indeed, officer.' He decided against tipping him.

The policeman nodded briefly and strolled on to check that traffic on the main road was moving satisfactorily.

Jack shut the window viciously, slid the gear-lever into second, placed the heel of his left shoe on the clutch, the toe on the brake, right foot hovering over the accelerator.

Where was Robina?

They were running late.

They never ran late.

16

Duggy jogged northward, keeping well under the canopy of young birch and willow trees by the lineside. A blackbird flew up in front of him, making a great commotion as he 'chuck-chuck-chucked' at Duggy from a safe distance. Duggy reflected that this was nothing to how disturbed the wildlife was going to be, once a regular train service was established.

He crouched behind a clump of gorse bushes near the Plenmellor bridge, at the beginning of the embankment, south of the Alston Arches. The wide curve was shaped like an opened-out hairpin.

There was a light grey van parked near the opposite point of the pin, near the end of the Arches. Men in overalls were carrying green boxes out of the back doors. His eyes narrowed as he read the black lettering on the side of the van: Tynedale TV. That was a new one on him. Interested now, he settled himself more comfortably and watched closely.

An outbreak of 'chucking' from the blackbird heralded the arrival of Tim and Cathy, followed by the Daler and its train. Duggy pointed to the grey van. They nodded and, without speaking, continued on their way, sliding down the embankment on to the road. Duggy turned to watch them running easily along to the old road bridge, Cathy's hair bouncing at every step. Looked as if they'd had a wash and tidy up—they had needed it.

The steam train continued down the line and into the station.

Duggy turned his attention back to the van. The TV crew were on the railway now, manhandling their gear up the embankment from the van. They must have official permission to be there. He couldn't very well cross the bridge when they were on it; he would wait until their cameras were set up and then run over before anybody realised.

Tim and Cathy disappeared over the river and under the railway to join the main road; they would be O.K. now. There was, he saw, a black police van parked near the end of the old bridge. If he kept his head down, behind the bushes along the top of the embankment, and behind the parapet wall on the Arches, he wouldn't be all that noticable.

Suddenly Duggy felt like shouting and jumping up and down, doing a dance along the track, when he thought of what Grandad had told him: Unicus lay concealed somewhere in the station. He felt he could concentrate on helping to track down the gang, now that he knew they hadn't got the loco— or his Dad.

Far away to his left, two small figures advanced down the steep hill towards Bellister Castle: Simon and Chas.

They would never find the gang. There wasn't enough time, really, when you thought about how spread out Haltwhistle was —all those lonnens and roads to check.

He wondered if Tim and Cathy had seen any of the gang yet, and hoped desperately that none of the gang had recognised them....

It was taking the TV men a long time—he wished they would hurry up. Hang on—they seemed to be burying something. Duggy breathed in sharply. They *were* burying something. His mind flashed back to Lambley viaduct. So they intended blowing up this viaduct too. Cold rage such as he had never experienced had him by the throat. The day of Unicus—the day his family had worked towards for years— was going to be shattered.

Suddenly Duggy didn't care if the entire membership of the Houses of Commons and Lords were shot by these terrorists.

All he cared about was Unicus. He imagined his Dad driving his new loco or his Grandad driving his old loco, over the Alston Arches, and then—bang! Everything blown up.

Why couldn't they leave everybody in peace? Yesterday Duggy's temper would have risen; he would have shouted a bit, thrown things, then gone off somewhere quiet until he cooled off, before going for help. Today his rage was cool and clear. He began to recognise the importance of not going at things like a bull at a gate.

There was a police van and, presumably, a policeman, at the far side of the bridge, out of sight of the TV van. If he made a run for it, cut the detonator wires, dodged past the men and their van, and collared the police....

He would be well on to the bridge before the men saw him. With luck they would be so busy they wouldn't see him, or they would assume that he was a railwayman

They were bound to be armed.

Duggy pulled a pair of wire-clippers from his boiler-suit pocket. He waited, watching the men on the viaduct.

They went through the motions of being a TV crew. They pointed the cameras at various objects; they panned the cameras round the line for the benefit of any onlookers.

At ten minutes to ten, they left their gear and returned to the van.

At five minutes to ten, they closed the rear doors and walked downriver for a hundred yards or so, to where they could see and be seen from the signal-box. One man knelt in the grass beside a small black box with his hand over the plunger, ready to detonate. A second man watched for Mr. Robinson's second handkerchief-wave.

The odds were now with Duggy.

He ran as he had never run; if he kept to the middle of the trackbed, he wouldn't be seen from below, up at this height.

He cut the detonator wires in two places, kept on along the embankment towards the station, then down and through the footpath tunnel, making for the Police van.

Panting, he opened the passenger door and fell into the seat.

'Quick!' Duggy gasped, pointing to the TV gear on the line. 'There's a gang of assassins back there!'

The uniformed driver turned towards him.

It was Ginger.

Ginger's face, still swollen and discoloured by bee stings, took on a vicious expression as he recognised Duggy. Clearly he thought he had seen the last of Duggy; he had not expected this kid to land in his lap—literally. On the one hand he owed Duggy one for his painful experience at Lambley. Instinctively Ginger touched his aching face. On the other hand, the boss and the rest of the gang thought that Duggy was securely bolted into Lambley station house; indeed, Ginger himself half-believed it.

You'd have thought a kid of Duggy's age would be too scared to do what he had done, knowing the TV crew to be gang members.

Any minute now Max would give the first signal to Robina the 'hit man', followed a few seconds later by the second signal to the crew near the viaduct. They would detonate the charge to divert the attention of the law and the folk on the station long enough for Max and other back-up men to reach the police van, which Ginger would then drive off to the next exchange vehicle, followed by the TV van.

And now this kid had shown up.

17

Shortly after nine-thirty, a workman in greasy-topped cap and overalls unlocked the end doors of the engine-shed. A narrow, sleek, black shape nosed out, was coupled to a matching set of carriages, and stood near the points. One or two people noticed it, but, without exception, the crowd expected the new power for the line to be a new steam loco in the style of Nigel Gresley.

Meanwhile a plume of steam appeared from behind the hill at Plenmellor siding.

Old Duggy eased the Daler and the coaches round the slow curve on to the Alston Arches. He noticed some men near the north end of the bridge climbing into a grey TV van. He eased off the throttle, on the look-out for trouble. In his day no 'civvies' would have been allowed near the line. His teeth clamped hard on his pipe. There was even somebody at the top of the signal-box steps, pestering Tot, like as not.

Leaning out of the cab, he watched for old Bas. There he was, on the Alston side platform, grinning like a cut melon. Old Duggy waved, pleased to see his fireman had made it in time . . . ALPS must have run him down by car. He likely wouldn't be too pleased at missing the run down from Alston. Still, Duggy had done not too badly, for a young 'un.He hoped old Bas had got the hang of that new-fangled radio-telephone they had to use until the signal-boxes were finished. You knew where you were with the old 'Tablet' system.

Unicus had to take second place today – the old 'un was the first on the Alston run . . . mind, he had nothing against the new loco, but man, he thought, there's nowt to beat steam.

Cameras clicked, flashed and zoomed, capturing the Daler and its billowing steam, the fluttering bunting and swaying flower-baskets touched by a light breeze, the sign: Haltwhistle for Alston.

Chas and Simon joined forces with Tim and Cathy on the station platform, mingling with the crowd round the VIPs, still hoping desperately to find out from which direction the threat would come.

They saw Duggy running along the Alston Arches.

They felt like screaming a warning to the VIPs who stood chatting along the edge of the platform, waiting.

Tired, tense and with a tight feeling of failure settling on them like a duvet, the four teenagers searched the crowd.

Chas noticed, without recognising, one man in particular: tall and rangy, wearing an Aran sweater and fawn trousers, his dark hair cropped so that he looked just like a spent match.

Of the gang there was no sign.

A middle-aged, bespectacled man in walking gear – socks turned over his boots; rucksack and anorak—leaned against the signal-box, gazing anxiously round the station. Chas wished he had had the nerve to ask Tot if they could watch from up there....

Suddenly Cathy grabbed his arm and shouted excitedly: 'Chas! It's him—that man up there on the signal-box steps.'

'Can't be—he's old. Our lot are all youngish.' Chas looked narrowly at Mr. Robinson. 'He's nothing like anybody I've seen.'

'Yes, but look at his feet—he's got his ankles crossed, just like that awful man at Alston. And I've never seen anybody else stand like that—you'd think he would fall over—'

Tim and Simon were already half-way up the steps before

Chas had finished contradicting Cathy. They didn't notice the spent-match man following close behind.

Mr. Robinson felt rather than saw them bounding up the wooden steps.

He recognised them—and guessed their intentions.

With one despairing glance at the Railway Hotel window, he leaped over the handrail. The bogus police van was waiting for him; he had checked earlier. Ginger would have the engine running.

He could still escape. He must escape.

Robina would just have to do the best she could—take out the targets and scarper in the Jaguar as planned. The operation, though not as smooth as one would have wished, would be successful.

Those blasted kids—

The 'police' van started to move.

Tim launched himself at Mr. Robinson's hiking-boots.

Mr. Robinson reached out to open the rear door,kicked out at Tim, grabbed hopelessly at air as Ginger, seeing what was happening through his wing-mirror, accelerated.

Simon bowled a fast left-arm half-brick at Mr. Robinson's rear.

Mr. Robinson turned a look of pure distilled hatred on him. Mrs. Waite would not have recognised him.

Cathy watched, white with excitement. They had done it!

The spent-match man pointed a revolver at Mr. Robinson's midriff.

'Well caught and bowled, lads,' he said tersely.

'Special Branch—you can go for your train ride now if you like. Everything's in hand here!' He lowered his voice, not taking his glance off Mr. Robinson. 'No need to spoil the celebrations—carry on as if nothing has happened. Don't suppose the public's noticed anything amiss. We'll be in touch!'

Meanwhile Ginger's van had careered off the narrow road: Duggy had seized his chance—and the steering-wheel.

Startled, Ginger took his gaze from the wing-mirror. Max, he realised with a shock, was copped.

'I knew I should've finished youse off at the start,' he snarled. 'And it's still not too late—' He aimed his revolver at the centre of Duggy's forehead.

Then Duggy was silhouetted against a shiny black, genuine police car as it pulled alongside.

Two armed uniformed policemen jumped out.

'Right you—gun on the floor and out!' one of them snapped, while the second one snatched at Ginger's door.

Ginger knew when he was licked.

Chas, on hearing Cathy's excited: 'It's him!' saw the despairing glance of Mr. Robinson, traced a trajectory and noticed a small round glistening circle in the open window of the Railway Hotel. Camera lens—or telescopic gun-sight?

He turned in mid-argument and, long legs flailing, jumped down and bounded over the main-line double track, disregarding the good-natured 'Heres' and 'Look outs' of the crowd as he pushed them aside. He streaked past the station car-park, across the road, past a policeman standing on the corner, holding an animated conversation on the RT.

In the hotel, Robina quickly weighed up her chances.

Max had gone. There was no sign of her targets. The sight of Chas loping over the road forced her decision. She grabbed her gun, tried and failed to push it into her bag, jettisoned it and ran for the stairs.

Jack had the car door open. She leapt in. The Jaguar roared into life and shot off in the direction of Hexham.

Chas watched it, with despair in his heart. He did not realise that the blonde and the small dark man from the red

Range Rover were the same person. Nor did he realise that Jack, the driver, was also the driver of the kidnap Land Rover.

He only knew that they had something to do with the gang, and they had escaped by seconds. He had not expected a woman.

Afterwards he wondered what on earth he expected to do if he had caught up with them....

Wearily, Chas approached the waiting policeman, who was, he saw, wearing a smug expression. The policeman had informed headquarters of the rapid departure of the Jaguar. It was followed to the Hexham farmhouse where a pantechnicon stood ready to whisk the Lestrange gang to Port Ryan.

'Now, lad,' the sergeant said genially to Chas. 'Running for a bus?'

Old Duggy was in his element; he couldn't remember when he last enjoyed himself so much. Masses of steam, and a little smoke, settled round the Daler as she chuntered alongside the Alston platform.

The cheering, laughing crowd disregarded the footbridge and surged across the main line to pay homage to the loco and train: to Steam.

The old enginemen pretended not to notice, but their caps were almost back to front, a sure sign of agitation. Finally they waved to the cameras, then retreated into the security of their cab.

Like a deferential handmaiden, Unicus waited politely, some distance from the steam loco.

'Isn't that something!' an American voice breathed. 'That's class!'

'A Concorde of the Rails,' one elderly gentleman called her.

Big Duggy listened, nodded, and wished he could start up; he was anxious to be away, but rules were rules; he had to wait.

This, he thought, was the old man's day.

He surveyed the instrument panel in front of him. Batteries were charged; everything in order. The cab was like a lab; no grime or oil or tea-cans here. Behind the cab, a narrow aisle down the centre of the loco was lined with black ceramic doors, behind which were the powerful batteries.

One half-turn of the master key and the engine would be ready to start.

Ordinary passengers climbed into Unicus's carriages and settled comfortably into the well-designed seats. Some of the VIPs would have preferred to travel in Unicus—especially the women. Unicus would deposit no smuts on May Day hats. But they knew their places, and boarded the steam train.

The chairman of ALPS, Alston Line Preservation Society, made a short, enthusiastic speech.

A green flag waved. The new Alston Line was open.

A railway official joined Old Duggy at the last minute, clutching a radio telephone.

'New-fangled rubbish!' Old Bas muttered.

The old loco put on another show of steam for the cameras as she climbed over the Alston Arches and round into Broomhouse cutting. At the three-mile post near Feather-stone, the official radioed back to Haltwhistle that they were now a safe distance and Unicus could follow on.

'Not that different from the old sections' old Bas commented, eyeing the official's performance.

Unicus glided away from Haltwhistle with a train full of passengers, seeming not to notice the incline. Big Duggy had a mental picture of old Bas shovelling coal on the Daler to raise enough steam to trundle up the incline. He retarded Unicus in case he overshot the three-mile safety gap. Young

Duggy, taking notice of how the controls worked, understood and grinned. Unicus was a winner. Chas and Tim, Simon and Cathy travelled in the aisle, between the banks of batteries.

'Interesting, but cramped,' Tim said, with a huge yawn.

'Dunno how Dug can raise enough energy to stand in the cab—he must be as shattered as we are. Expect the adrenalin's flowing or something,' Simon commented. He patted the smooth ceramic door against which he leaned, almost too tired to stand unsupported. 'It's O.K., isn't it? Not what I expected.'

'Great,' Tim agreed. 'You hardly know you're moving on rails at all. Compared with the racket and smoke on the Daler—well, it's like comparing a Rolls with a Ford eight.'

Cathy came to life at the criticism of the old loco.

'Don't you dare insult the Daler! It was great. You can't deny that you lot enjoyed it as well, steaming down to Plenmellor on the hotplate.'

Nobody bothered to correct Cathy's 'hotplate'; they were silent until Unicus slid into Slaggyford.

The station was crammed with people, some trying to board the train, others taking pictures or merely admiring the new loco.

Feeling flat after their eventful weekend, the four waved to driver Big Duggy and son, and turned to climb wearily up the homeward hill, breathing in the fresh, sweet air, remembering the homework they had to finish for Tuesday . . .

'Tuesday. That's tomorrow,' Cathy wailed. 'It can't be—we've got nothing done this weekend. Our folks'll be absolutely raving mad.'

'Ours'll not be too chuffed either,' Tim admitted cheerfully.

They were both right.

There were repercussions and reproaches, congratulations

and condemnations. But, as Mr. Tate said, 'It's like water off a duck's back. Those two bairns of ours will never change.'

Now it was July.

The Cubbys and Tates sprawled on a patch of sheep-nibbled turf on the fells above Slaggyford, gazing up at the summer sky. Cathy rested a sunburnt arm over her eyes, then she turned over on to her stomach, waving her feet in the air.

'Keep still, can't you?' Simon complained. 'You're making a draught.'

Cathy sighed from sheer undiluted pleasure. 'Isn't it just lovely to be here—to be just ordinary again?'

'Nobody'll ever want to kidnap us again after the show we put up on May Day. And did I tell you that Mam and Dad've threatened to lock Si and me in the apple loft with a bucket of water and a couple of loaves, if we get into any more bother? I don't think we will. From now on we'll lead happy, useful lives, and live and die here among the sheep—same as our folks have done for centuries, like the Men of Alston Moor.'

'Oh—here we go again. Shut up and don't talk soft,' Simon retorted. 'It's far too hot to bother—and anyway, how do we know where we'll end up?'

'There's a lot of things ended up in peculiar places, like those soup cups—remember—at Alston? You know,' Cathy nudged Simon. 'Stuffed in the exhaust of that Range Rover.' She grew more and more exasperated as the others pretended not to understand.

'Ah!' Tim sat up suddenly and said dramatically: 'You mean the paper cup and bacon sandwich bags with "Duggy's Tea" printed all over, which the police found in the exhaust of a new red Range Rover, put there by persons unknown. A valuable clue, the law reckoned. Why, they asked themselves, had a group of law-abiding, soup-loving, anti-litter teenagers felt obliged to vandalise a harmless Range Rover? Yes—it was funny about that.... '

'You're a clown, Tim Cubby!' Cathy laughed. 'But all the same, it was lucky the police found the Rover—or they would never have found the bags and connected them with us.'

'That wasn't luck. What d'ye call him—Max—actually went to the police in Hexham and told them it had been stolen, from "a friend"! It was a decoy, like we said,' Tim explained.

'Well, I still think it was lucky,' Cathy insisted.

'It was that bobby I nearly knocked over when I tried to catch the gunman or woman in the Railway Hotel—apparently he was at Hexham on the day Max reported the Rover missing, and he noticed the Jaguar, Max's car, because its number was the same as his or something—his initials, I mean! And the number was his kid's birthday, so he remembered it, and when the police connected the Rover with our kidnap, because of the sandwich-bags—well, he smelt a rat, realised the Jag might be involved as well,' Chas added thoughtfully; 'Funny, the gunman being a woman. I could've nabbed her, you know, but I didn't expect a blonde. And then, if I had caught her, the police might not have traced the Jag to that farm at Hexham.'

'Clever,' Tim said. 'Devious. Prefect timing—but still it didn't work.'

'And it was only two little things that spoiled their plot—the Jag number plate, and the funny way that awful man stood. Nobody would've found them, but for that,' Cathy said, then amended generously: 'Well, *we* wouldn't—the police might have....'

'The funniest thing about the whole affair is the thought of all that cash stashed away in Geneva, while Lestrange's mob will be in jail for years, so they can't get at it—and neither can whoever paid Lestrange to kill the VIPs.'

Simon grinned. 'It sort of makes it worthwhile.'

They pondered on justice for a while, then: 'Heard the latest?' Tim asked.

'Well, we don't know if what we know is the latest till you tell us,' Cathy said. 'So, come on, tell us.'

Having riveted their attention, Tim announced: 'Duggy's got a job—BR trainee driver. Left school—just like that. He'll be going on to Unicus, I'll bet, when he's qualified.'

They sat up, leaning back on their elbows to discuss the news.

'Well, we saw that coming,' Simon said. 'Lucky beggar—knowing what he wants to do—and doing it.' He stared across the valley, watching cloud shadows move slowly over Williamston Fell.

Chas eyed him but said nothing. Tim flicked a pebble into the burn; they watched the widening ripples.

'What d'ye mean—lucky? He's worked at it. You aren't thinking of being a loco driver, are you, Si?' Tim was serious for once.

'Not likely! Cars, mebbe, but not locos.' Simon answered slowly. 'S'ppose I'll end up on the farm.... '

'Well, it's not the end of the world, is it? What's wrong with farming? A lot of folks'd give their eye teeth for the chance,' Cathy said, irritated that Simon wanted to change things. She had noticed that, for all her posh parents and presents, Melly hadn't half the fun that she herself had. Still, she had enjoyed her visits to Melly's house.

'There's a lot of mechanical engineering work on a farm, you know,' Chas said. 'All that machinery to repair and maintain—you know how things always conk out when you most need them. Plenty of scope there—keep your Dad happy, too.'

'True,' Simon agreed gloomily. 'Yes, you're right. You two have no problems—now that your Dad's taken up proper farming.' Chas opened his mouth to speak, then closed it and glanced quickly at Tim.

For scientific research purposes, their Dad's farm was going organic, but he didn't want it broadcast yet, in case it wasn't a success.

'We haven't had our exam results yet,' Cathy said, in a doom-laden voice.

'For Pete's sake, let's talk about something else. I mean—exams, in the middle of the holidays.'

'You're right, Si, it's just the start—July—we've got all those weeks and weeks to do nothing in,' Cathy said dreamily.

Perversely, nobody could think of anything to say, until the distant whistle of Unicus drifted up from the level-crossing.

'That reminds me—did you see about ALPS changing its name?' Tim said, watching the narrow, black torpedo-shape glide down the line past Duggy's house.

'Change ALPS to something else, you mean? Seems a bit daft to me. I mean ALPS is a good name—snappy—Alston Line Pres—'

'No, idiot!' Tim interrupted Cathy; he sprinkled a large handful of grass over her hair. 'Unicus! They've changed it—they thought Unicus wasn't quite right—it doesn't mean much to most folks.'

'It doesn't mean anything to me,' Simon admitted. 'Sounds like something out of one of those legends they used to read out to us on Friday afternoons in the infants'. Unicus sounds like something with a lot of heads.'

'It actually means unparalleled, unique—that sort of thing. Like the Rainhill Trials, you know,' Chas informed them. 'Unpariel—or was it Nonpariel? Can't remember offhand.'

'Oh, yes, that explains everything. Thanks very much.' Tim wnked at Simon.

'Well, ask Duggy then. It was Duggy who came up with Unicus in the first place, reckoned it was appropriate,' Chas said.

'Didn't know Duggy knew any Latin,' Tim said.

'Didn't know you knew any.'

'Looked it up in a dictionary—ages ago.' And Tim added graciously: 'But you explained it pretty well—couldn't have done better meself.'

'You never know, with Duggy,' Simon said.

'You never know with anybody,' Chas said. Fancy Tim looking things up in a Latin dictionary . . .

'It strikes me,' Cathy said, still picking grass out of her hair, 'that our Latin is about as good as our English: not very. Come on, then, what's the new name? What've they called it? Alston Express or something?'

'Yes, that's it—something.'

'Oh, well, if you're going to be funny –' Cathy pretended to be huffed.

'Try again,' Chas suggested.

'Erm—Black Peril?' Simon said, his interest waning rapidly.

'Well, no.... Duggy mentioned to ALPS committee about Cathy calling it the Midnight Line, when we were fooling about on the old railmotor, and they thought: what a good idea—you know, with the loco being black . . . '

'Tum—te—tum!' Tim hummed, aggravating everybody, as he intended. 'So, we've established that the loco is black. Pay attention, you lot—there may be more revelations.'

'Look, are you going to tell us, Chas Cubby, or have we to wring it out of you?' Simon said, exasperated. 'I mean, I know we've got all summer and nothing to do—except the hay, which Dad's cutting tomorrow, with this fine weather. Then there's the baler to patch up—again—and there's the shop to help in, for them as wants extra pocket-money. And there's masses of reading and revision to do for next term. No,we've nothing to do.'

Cathy sat up at the mention of extra pocket-money.

Chas drew a small box from his pocket, and with a grand flourish, presented it to Cathy.

'This, Duggy said to tell you, when he gave it to me last night, is to replace your old ALPS badge, which you hadn't missed—had you? You lost it in the kerfuffle in May. The police found it, on the Kirkhaugh road—thought it must have been pulled off your jacket, the day you disappeared. Lucky you scratched your initials on the back, wasn't it? They found other clues too: a bit of torn denim, footprints,tyre marks—all sorts of little things. You see, Duggy's Mum told the Law everything, as soon as Duggy hung the phone up. The police kept their heads down, so as not to alarm the gang. Anyway, they kept them down so far that they didn't know where we were, till we turned up at Haltwhistle station. They were more interested in catching the brains behind Lestrange—they thought we might lead the police to their leader, if you see what I mean, only it was too late.... '

'What d'ye mean—too late?' Cathy asked, dismayed. 'You mean it's not finished yet? But I thought they'd caught the lot—the whole gang, at the farm at Hexham. They said—'

Chas shook his head. 'No—the main one escaped—and some of the others who live, or lived, locally. The police reckon they could still be here somewhere. There'll be no evidence against them, I suppose. There's been more to it than we'll ever know.'

'The gang knew so much about everybody—they must have had loads of people planted. Max and the blonde were sort of section leaders—pretty high up, but not the boss.'

Suddenly the day seemed less bright.

'So the gang boss'll get his money after all—after all our struggles to catch him—them.... we might as well not have bothered.' Cathy stared miserably at the jewel box.

'No, silly—the VIPs escaped, didn't they? Nobody's going to pay when the gang's bodged the job. We stopped the blonde from shooting them all. That's the main thing—nobody hurt, really.'

'But Chas—just think—we might never know who the rest of the gang are. They could be anywhere. You know, I still have nightmares about being on Lambley viaduct when Duggy cut the shot-wires—remember? And afterwards everybody thought we were romancing 'cos somebody had pinched the gelignite, and there was no sign left of anything.'

'Aye,' Simon grinned at his sister. 'It was nearly funny, wasn't it? You going on about jelly, and Duggy doing his nut. It was just as well he pocketed the wire he cut off—else the Police would never have believed our story. I say—' Suddenly Simon sat up; the others stared at him. 'I wonder who did take the geli and shot wires out of the viaduct?'

Cathy gasped.

'Could have been the same chap who let Chuck out of Bas's shed.'

'There's still a mystery or two left to solve, what with people going away and pinching geli and plans and parking trailers in people's gardens,' Chas said, then he yawned and lay back again and closed his eyes. 'Tell you what,' he murmured. 'We'll let somebody else sort it out. They'll all disappear when they think everybody's forgotten about the affair. The police said they usually do that. So anybody who moves away is a suspect. That reminds me—we never gave the Kings anything in exchange for our breakfasts—remember all that food Duggy doled out that Sunday morning? They've moved, but nobody would suspect them of anything nasty—canny couple, Duggy said they were. Seriously though, I did wonder about M—'

Simon kicked Chas's purple-socked, bony ankle, and in the resulting mêlée, Chas's words left Cathy wondering, too. She cast an extremely old-fashioned glance at Chas but said nothing. She had thought it strange at the time that Melly and her parents had moved away without a word to anybody, then only last week, a postcard from Brasilia had arrived at Burnhaugh adressed to Cathy, and signed 'Melly'. No message, just 'Melly'.

After a long silence, in which Chas massaged his ankle, Cathy asked of nobody in particular: 'I wondered, too, about my handlebar grip—you know the one? Well, Melly was supposed to find it on the ashy path at Lambley, but how did it get there? My bike was in the trailer, so it couldn't have fallen out of that, could it? And the ashy path is too narrow for a Land Rover, so my bike would never be near there. So—where did Melly get it from? And when? And why?' She gazed from one to the other with her notorious bland expression.

Cathy strikes again, thought Simon. Aloud, he said: 'Well, it's only in books that all the loose ends are tied up. In real life, you just never know. I mean, we'll never know where Big Duggy's blueprints went. They were all bundled up in a tube, addressed to the Bank, and we forgot to put it through Millie's door—it was too big for the post-box.'

They thought for a while, then Simon spoke again.

'Talking of Big Duggy—you know all that railway stuff Duggy and I told you he had in his front room?' They all nodded, grinning. 'Well, he must have given it to the ALPS museum at Alston. Saw it the other day. Everything seems to be there, fishbelly rail—the lot.'

'That's great,' Tim said.

'Listen, are you going to open that box, or not?' Chas demanded, creating a diversion. 'We're all a bit sick of mysteries; let's just get on with things and forget about Lestrange.' He collapsed on to the ground and shut his eyes, then half-opened them.

Cathy opened the lid. The others watched various expressions cross her face. She would never make a poker player, Chas thought.

'Oh! It's lovely.' Cathy gasped, flushing with surprise and pleasure. 'Look.' The boys crowded round, and looked. 'It's a silver brooch. Real silver.'

'It's black,' Simon pointed out. 'Silver's not black. It's—well—silver....'

'It's black enamel on silver, idiot.' Cathy peered closely at the brooch. 'And the silver nameplate says—' She looked up, beaming. 'It says : Midnight. It's a tiny model of Unicus—I mean, Midnight.'

'You really can't win, can you?' Chas said. 'They rename it specially for Cathy's convenience, and she still calls it Unicus. Mind you, I never thought that Unicus would catch on. Now Midnight—that's much snappier.'

They all laughed.

'Well—we all know, don't we,' Cathy said briskly, waving a hand towards the line. 'From the start, this was, and it always will be—The Midnight Line.'